Born with a Beard

Ted Ringer

Illustrations by George Peters

First Wonderful World Publishing edition, April 2006
Copyright © 2006 by Ted Ringer

Design: Katie Elliott
Illustrations: George Peters
Published in the United States by Wonderful World Publishing
Longmont, Colorado
USA
www.wonderfulworldpublishing.com

ISBN-10: 0-9777950-0-4
ISBN-13: 978-0-9777950-0-0

Library of Congress Control Number
2006901268

Printed in Canada

Table of
Contents

Chapter 1

Born with a Beard

I was born with a beard. This
was not something I had planned on. I didn't
know how or why it was. It was just there. It was
the first thing they noticed about me.

The doctor, although a professional, almost
dropped me. The nurses stared and, behind their
face masks, their jaws dropped open. I looked
around and instead of the pleasant and welcoming
looks I had been expecting, I saw shock, dismay,
bewilderment, and fear. Even on my parents' faces.
I cried.

This broke the spell that my entrance had caused.
My parents, though puzzled, instinctively comforted
me as they looked at each other for support. Later,

they drove me home from the hospital and, when they thought I was sleeping, I heard my father say, "Nobody in my family was born with a beard. Heck, I didn't even shave until I was nineteen.

As he finished saying this he took his eyes off the road and looked pointedly at my mother. She responded, "Well, no one in my family was like that. We were all girls."

My father was a businessman and he wasn't about to accept that. He said, "What about your mother's mustache?"

My mother drew her breath in sharply and told him to keep his eyes on the road.

My father had a sense of humor, but sometimes he didn't get far with it.

When we got home, they propped me up in a chair and took a good look at me. I was looking at them, too. Dad had a serious expression on his face like he had just eaten something he regretted. He was what I took to be tall, with just a hint of trouble around the middle. This he hid fairly well with a cardigan sweater. His hair was dark with streaks of white and, unlike his son, he was clean-shaven. His hands were folded as if in prayer, in front of his face. For all I knew, he was praying. I liked him.

I liked the way Mom looked, too. She had a wonderful kind of glow to her. Her hair was the color of my beard but with tiny, elegant streaks of gray through it. She looked sophisticated in her cotton suit but, as she looked at me, she couldn't keep herself from giggling and making little hiccuping noises. I responded with noises of my own, which she found charming.

She said to my father, "You see, he's just like a real baby."

To me, she said, "Goo, goo, goo."

I could have done without the goo, goo, goo, but that's how she was. Her eyes were bright and they shone at me, her baby boy. She looked good for just having had a baby with a beard, and I loved her. I was confident that we would make a happy family.

Just as this soothing thought settled on me, a small child walked into the room. This was my sister and, as she came closer, I reached out my arms to her. I was grateful to have a playmate and I mumbled a message of welcome to her.

She shrieked, "Mom, he's got a beard!" and hid behind my father.

My mother said, "Of course he's got a beard. He's your father's son."

Dad wasn't laughing.

My sister would not stop. She said, "But he's an animal. He's like a dog."

At the time, I wasn't vain, but I knew I was not an animal and tried to say so. I growled something at my sister and she hid her face.

My father decided that it was time he took control. He did so in an odd way. He began by clearing his throat quite loudly. Not just a preparatory

"Ahem," but a long drawn-out clearing of his throat and perhaps his mind. It was, in its own way, commanding. He sounded like a bear.

Finally, he said, "This is not an animal. This is your baby brother."

My sister, who had, by this time, regained her usual unchildlike composure said, "But Dad, look at his face. That is not the face of a baby. What are we going to call him? Mr. Baby? Grandpa Baby?"

My mother, who was always understanding and who also had a firm grip on reality said, "This is the only brother you have," and here she looked at my father, "and most likely the only brother you will have. He has a beard. I admit that is unusual, but it must be for a reason."

"Yeah," my sister said, " to save on bibs."

My mother, without acknowledging my sister's contribution, continued, "We don't know what that reason is, but I'm sure, over time, it will become clear. He's too young to shave, so we're just going to have to get used to it."

My father was nodding his head.

"Your mother is right. We don't know why he's like this, but you have to admit it's a pretty good beard. Not quite Santa Claus, but respectable. Dashing in its own way. Revolutionary."

My mother stiffened, "It's not funny."

Dad looked at my sister, who only raised her eyebrows, knowing any comment from her would be unwelcome.

I looked at the three of them and wished that I had the words to tell them that it didn't matter if I had a beard; I was one of them. They were looking intently at me and I could see they were doubtful, but I felt happy. I was home and with my family and somehow it would all work out. At least, they had no intention of returning me to the hospital.

Just then my sister suggested, "Maybe we could take him back?"

Mom looked over at my sister and turned the parental spotlight on her, saying, "This is your brother. He's small now but someday he will be bigger than you. You might find it wise to be nice to him." She added, "Plus, behind that beard is probably a great little baby."

I nodded vigorously and almost fell off the chair.

Chapter 2

Life Goes On

As the days went by, we all got used to each other. Dad appeared, at cribside, when he returned from his job in the city, going, "Ho, ho, ho," and laughing. He thought he was pretty funny. I laughed, too. Any middle-aged man going "Ho, ho, ho," is comical. He would then disappear into his den for cocktails.

My mother continued in the goo, goo, goo vein, but sometimes forgot I was a baby and begin to talk to me as if we were old friends. She would tell me the news: Eisenhower as president, Minneapolis in for more snow, and she would list the possibilities for my future: scholar, civic leader, head of a family. She then remembered the beard and, for her, the grand future faltered a little. She continued a bit shakily, but bravely: circus performer, sailor, mountain climber.

My sister also visited me. She had her own style. She'd walk with exaggerated slowness to the crib, while stroking her cheeks. She would then peer over, and say, "Grandpa, we're not getting any younger," and run out of the room squealing. She really was funny, I thought, and I was reassured by her words. If I got any younger, I would be out of business.

A baby, even one with a beard, is something to show off, and my parents, once they had recovered from the shock of my appearance, took me first to meet my grandparents. They met us at the door.

Winter is cold in Minnesota, and I was bundled up tight as protection against it. Mom carried me inside, and when she unwrapped me, it became obvious that I was not an ordinary child. My grandparents had been eagerly leaning over me, but then the first of my whiskers were revealed, and they drew back in shock. My grandmother gasped. My grandfather began clearing his throat. We waited.

He began, "A baby is a blessing." He stopped here and looked around uncertainly. We were all focused on him. The snow stopped momentarily and the clock ceased ticking, in anticipation of his remarks. He continued, "As we can all see, this is a very mature and, I'm sure, a very special baby and I am very glad to welcome him into the family." He smiled then, and we sighed in unison. The snow resumed and time went on as before.

My sister muttered, "I can't believe it."

My grandmother bent over and rubbed her cheek against my beard, murmuring, "What a big boy you are. Just like your father." Dad quickly looked at her, wondering just exactly what she meant, but softened when he saw Grandma's eyes twinkling.

He straightened and said, "Yes, we quite like him."

The afternoon progressed pleasantly as my grandfather told us stories of when he had been a baby. My parents, my grandmother, and my sister and I all nodded our heads as he told of traveling with his father, my great-grandfather, who everyone referred to as the

Chief, because of his close ties with the Indians. My grandfather had been at various Indian social events and had been one of a long line of papooses that circled the campfire during warm nights under the stars.

He also told how, as a baby, he had been able to read and had particularly liked Jules Verne, Dumas, and Tolstoy. He pointed to his glasses and said, "That's how I got these." My sister questioned his ability to remember that far back. He looked at me and winked, saying, "Some of us can remember."

He then walked to the bookshelves that lined the room and, after a moment, pulled out a small, slim volume. He came over to me and said, "This book meant a lot to me when I was your age, and I would like you to have my copy. Books can take us to worlds beyond our own and are an ocean on which we can set sail and explore the past and the future. Always keep them near you, for whether you read them or not, the potential within them will comfort you." He then indicated his glasses and added, "But be sure you have good light." He slipped the book between my blankets and when I got home, I found that it was a copy of The Odyssey in the original Greek.

The more I got to know this family, the better I liked them. Even my sister. She teased me and attempted to torment me, but I saw that she really did love me, despite everything, and she seemed to me to be the most entertaining of them all. She even began to like my beard and though she would never say so, I think at times, she wished she had one herself.

She sat beside me one afternoon and said, "When I grow up, I'm going to be the most powerful woman in France."

I smiled at her ambitious nature and then started humming the Marseillaise. We giggled and plotted and waited for spring.

Mom was doing a little plotting of her own. Based on all she had seen of me so far, she had great plans. Though I was barely in diapers, she had enrolled me in a school where she said I would learn 'What's what and what's not.' She hadn't quite figured out the exact route or roster of my carpool yet, but she was working on it.

Meanwhile, Dad was down in his den reading *The Wall Street Journal*. Every now and then we would hear a chuckled "Ho, ho, ho" float up the stairs, so we knew he was all right. One evening, he brought me down there to what he called, "The Inner Sanctum." Just the two of us. I had never been there before and though it was dark and dank, I found it exciting. There were books covering the walls, a couple of large chairs, and a globe that seemed life-size to me. A small, smoky fire burned in the fireplace.

We sat opposite each other in front of the fire in our big chairs. We should have been smoking cigars. He looked at me for a long time and I returned his gaze and wondered what was coming. He began to clear his throat. When that was all over, he leaned forward and said, "When you are a little bit older, if you want to, it would make me very happy if you would come to work for me. With me, as my partner. You don't have to say anything now. Just think it over."

Of course, I was touched and proud that he would want me. I imagined us together in a big office, our desks facing each other across an elegantly carpeted expanse. There were maps on the walls, a big globe stood by the window, and the phones were ringing constantly. In between signing huge deals, we smiled at each other. He gave me the thumbs up sign and I returned it, confident that business was good to us and that we were good for business.

I looked up from my reverie to see my father smiling kindly at me. Though just a little baby, it seemed I had a lot to look forward to -- a wonderful education at an exclusive school, a brilliant career in business, and powerful connections in France. I wouldn't have changed places with any other baby in the world, beard or no beard.

Chapter 3

We Listen To Music

One of the things I soon learned about my family was that they loved to listen to music. Each Sunday, after what seemed to me to be a huge breakfast of bacon, toast, and eggs or, as a special treat for my sister, French toast, my father, with much preparatory groaning, would lie down on the couch with his feet up and his arm thrown over his eyes. My mother went to the walnut box in the corner and put on a record. On Sundays, it was always classical music -- Beethoven, Brahms, Tchaikovsky, Schumann. It was a romantic household. My sister sat under the table with her books and I lounged in my crib, while the warm winter sunshine poured through the windows.

With Dad on the couch, immobile, the music alternately floated toward us or attacked us or surprised us, but it always took us to another time and another place, far away from Minnesota. We lay there for hours. Mom flipped the records and, while we were listening, she cleaned the kitchen. Her kind of music was musicals.

Although I knew it was just a song, it gave me a pang, thinking of my future business partner, to hear her sing so enthusiastically about washing that man right out of her hair. My sister was into Maurice Chevalier, Josephine Baker, and Edith Piaf. I had a radio by my crib and my favorites were "Venus in Bluejeans," Brenda Lee, and Marty Robbins.

My father was the one most affected by this Sunday music. He had performed in operas during the time he spent in college. He was what they call a spear carrier. This sounded important and I imagined him waiting anxiously, in the wings, with his spear towering over everything. He was dressed in one of those Fuller Brush helmets with a leather vest, weird short pants, and sandals with thongs twining up his legs.

He heard his cue and marched, all alone, to the center of the stage singing in his deep bass -- "Ho, ho , ho." He then turned serenely toward stage left and made a dignified exit. The crowd went wild. Bouquets of exotic flowers were thrown at the stage. Earnest cries of "Bravo" showered down from the cheap seats. The audience would not allow the performance to continue until it had rewarded him. He was called back to the stage. He marched out to thunderous applause, acknowledged his well-wishers, and modestly departed. His future in opera was a bright one, but he had his education to think of and was possessed by a driving ambition to become a businessman.

He did pursue a career in business, but his love for music remained with him and so, each Sunday, he could be found on the couch. Every now and then, as he lay there, his inert form would jerk and sounds emerged from him, as if from a dream. My sister and I looked at each other and nodded our heads, glad to know that our father's life was big enough to contain a place for Opera.

My mother, on the other hand, was always washing that man out of her hair or else becoming accustomed to his face. We worried about her, but when she wasn't singing she seemed just like the Mom she had been before.

One day I was relaxing in my crib, reading. I heard my father singing, down in the den. Although he loved music, it was rare to actually hear him sing anything. The words drifted up to me …

> In my adobe hacienda
> There's a touch of Mexico
> Cactus much lovelier than orchids
> Blooming in the patio

I was fascinated. As he sang, the melody took me to another place. A place near the desert where the light was always changing and where there wasn't any snow. I knew instinctively that this was another kind

of romance and I wanted to be part of it. I closed my eyes and saw myself riding toward an impossibly distant horizon, my beard flowing in the breeze.

I was not riding aimlessly through the great West. I had a destination. I was headed for Rosa's cantina, where there was a girl I knew. Granted, not a very nice girl, but she was beautiful, and to dance with her was as close to heaven as this cowboy could imagine. Plus, the food at Rosa's was great -- Hot Dogs, fries, and shakes. No baby food there and the bottles they served weren't warm; they were cold and full of sugar.

I tied my pony to the rail outside and made my stiff-legged way through the swinging doors. It was quite a lively crowd for a school night. In the corners were poker games that looked like they had been going on for some time. The bar was full and an unhealthy-looking guy was playing the piano, while a few couples danced. I bellied up to the bar and looked around.

The bartender came over and said, "Nice beard. What'll it be?"

I looked at him closely to see if he was mocking me. He wasn't. "Vanilla shake," I said, "and hurry it up. I've been in the saddle all day."

He returned with the shake, and I downed half of it in one gulp. It had been a while since I had had one, and I immediately got one of those pains in my forehead. I didn't want anyone to think I was a greenhorn, so I stood there in motionless agony with a look I hoped might pass for a smile.

From beside me a sweet, dark voice said, "Hey stranger, you don't look so good."

I gasped and said, "Don't bother me. I'm thinking."

I then opened my eyes and saw her there, that

wicked Felina, the girl that I loved.

She smiled at me, said, "See you later," and walked out into the crowd and up to the biggest, meanest guy I had ever seen. They began to dance.

I don't know if it was love or the shake or the long ride or what, but I saw red. I knew she didn't love me and probably didn't love anyone, but I wasn't going to let her dance with that brute. I went up to them, in the middle of the dance floor, and cut in. The big guy stood there for a moment fuming and then grabbed me and lifted me off the floor, with a loud, frightening growl.

Everyone stopped and looked at us. The piano was silent. The only sounds were my spurs turning slowly, three feet off the ground.

"Why don't you go back to your Mama?" he snarled. "Of course, she probably thought you were a dog, not her baby boy."

He turned to the crowd and laughed.

His breath was terrible. My beard quivered. I passed over the remark about my mother and said,

"You must have said Roy, not boy. No one calls me boy." I gave him the worst look I had.

It wasn't bad enough.

He carried me outside to my pony, put me in the saddle, and said, "Git. And don't come back until you're old enough."

"Old enough for what?" I asked, defiant to the end.

I glanced at Felina, in the doorway, and through her giggles she waved sweetly to me. I made a silent vow to return. At that instant, the big galoot smacked the back of the pony with his six-shooter, and I was on my way into the night.

A little ways down the trail, my pony stumbled badly, and it jolted me out of my disappointment and shame. I noticed that it was light out and a song was running through my head...

When setting sun says the long day is done
Sweet music starts to fill the air
In my adobe hacienda,
Life and Love are everywhere

I raised my head and there was my father looking down at me. He was smiling and he said, "Well, old timer, how about a bottle?"

Chapter 4

At Play In The Kitchen

My mother was not a large woman, but she did love to cook. She had other talents, but she loved to mess around in the kitchen. Everyone in our family liked to eat. In fact, it was almost a necessity, so we provided her with an appreciative audience and handy guinea pigs on which she could try out her recipes.

My mother not only made such Midwestern staples as fish sticks, pot roast, and meatloaf, she also experimented with little-known dishes from all over the world. We sometimes thought they might be from out of this world.

I couldn't pronounce the names of even a fraction of what she lovingly prepared for us, but my father would act as if he could. Whether he knew what it was or not, and he would say, "Dear, this is the best Despratzabuli casserole I think I've ever had." or "This roasted Tigwinkle is wonderful, Honey." He'd then lift his fork with whatever it was on it, in a gesture of tribute and respect, and my mother would blush. My sister could pronounce, with elegance, any concoction remotely French. I sat, in my high chair, equipped with a bottle full of the same old exotic formula she had whipped together earlier, smiled down on my happy and well-fed family, and felt a little envious.

When Mom began to prepare dinner in the late afternoon, she liked to have me with her in the kitchen. There she brought an army of bowls and utensils to bear on the contents of our refrigerator. She explained to me what she was doing as she went along, and I learned a lot about cooking this way. She kept cookbooks in a glass cupboard next to the oven. I had never seen her actually read these books, but she seemed to know everything in and about them.

One day, she decided that it was time for me to try

my hand at making up a recipe. She and I were the
only ones home. My father had taken my sister with
him to look at factories. This was a businessman's idea
of fun. As they drove around, he'd say to her, "That
one must be 80,000 square feet." And she would nod
her head, sagely, and say, "Yep. And it's beautiful, too."
I had never been on one of these expeditions, but I
was assured by my sister that my time would come.

Anyway, my mother and I were going to make
something. She brought out everything in the refrigerator and opened all the cupboard doors. Although
I had no idea what most of this stuff was, it was my
job to pick the ingredients with which we were going
to make dinner. Do I underestimate when I say that
my mother had an
adventurous soul?

I first pointed
to a large package.
This turned out
to be hamburger.
So far, so good. I

then indicated the orange juice. I followed this with some cream cheese, three eggs, strawberry jam, and a head of lettuce. So much for the entreé, as my sister would say. From the spice rack, I selected basil, curry, and a small bottle of vanilla. We put all this into a large bowl and sat back for a moment to contemplate our next move.

Mom winked and said, "This will be something truly different."

She asked if she could make a suggestion. I nodded.

"I think we should have some plain old peas and carrots on the side to keep things grounded."

I agreed whole-heartedly. One must always keep in mind for whom one is cooking, no matter how exciting it gets in the kitchen.

We mixed, we combined, we tossed, and we folded the contents of the big bowl into a suitable pan. I let Mom work the stove. She was neatness itself in the kitchen and, after we had safely gotten our dish into the oven, she cleaned up so that we would have a clear field for preparing dessert. This was a lesson I was determined to carry with me into the future -- always to be ready for dessert.

She arranged the dessert ingredients and, once more, I selected. There was flour and sugar and butter. This was the foundation on which we built what would soon become the dessert never to be forgotten in our family mythology. I, then added apples, vinegar, eggs, a jar of ovaltine, raisins, half a box of Cheerios, a package of Jello, and four marshmallows. For this, we brought out the mixer. Minutes later, in four cake pans, was what we hoped my sister would consider the piece dé resistánce.

We placed it in the oven with the other stuff. We smiled at each other, now something more than mother and son, though that was no small matter. We were now colleagues, partners, accomplices.

Mom cleaned up, and by the time the table was set, things in the kitchen were beginning to smell. And smelled great, we decided.

Mom looked around conspiratorially and whispered to me, "We'll tell them that this is your recipe, but we won't tell them what's in it."

I nodded. This would be our secret and, no matter what we were offered, we would never reveal, to any casually interested party nor to any great chef, what exactly had gone into the making of it.

When our dish was served, in the glow of candle-light, my father and my sister looked at each other and at the unusual-looking dish before them.

Dad asked innocently, "What is it?"

Mom said simply, "Just something your son and I cooked up this afternoon."

We both looked modestly at our creation.

Dad nodded uncertainly but lifted the first forkful to us and said, "It looks to me like a very tasty Beard-ed Scarpetto."

Mom and I had not thought to name it and were very pleased by this development.

My sister said, "It looks kind of weird. You go first."

Dad placed this first forkful in his mouth and began chewing. We all watched from the edge of our chairs. The candle flickered. He made a noise, with his mouth full, that could have been "uummm." His eyes rolled back into his head. No one moved.

He swallowed suddenly and said, "This really is good," and continued feeding with enthusiasm.

My sister looked closely to see if he was kidding and then tentatively tried a bite. She tried another. Even she started making noises.

Mom and I smiled proudly and Mom said, "Just wait until you try dessert."

Chapter 5

I Venture Outside

Having a beard was not the stigma you might think. Mom acted as if it were the most natural thing in the world. After the baby's bath, one brushed his beard. And it was a nice beard. Not a wispy thing that seemed about to fall off the face, but a full one in a deep chestnut color and with a shape that emphasized my baby eyes and broad forehead.

My father took the existence of my beard in stride and as simply a part of my growing up, but he was always amused by it. Its presence appealed to his sense of history, and he made little jokes about it and called me by the names of various famous beard growers -- Moses, General Sherman, King Richard.

My sister let me know in many ways that, despite the fact that I was her brother, she considered me just a bit odd. This didn't bother me. I liked her. I looked up to her. How could I help it? She was twice my size. I figured I could learn from her mistakes. It seemed to me that parents, even my parents, had probably always been old but that my sister had once been young like myself and had been through many of the things I knew to be in my future. She had started school. She had lost some of her teeth. She had successfully negotiated a later bedtime. She was on her way. Hey, she could walk.

I loved and admired her, even though I hadn't told her so, and I would have done anything for her. So when she came to me one day and said she wanted to show me something and that it was outside, I was very excited to see what it was.

Babies don't get to go outside much. We sleep a lot, we eat about every ten minutes, and everyone always wants to know how we are doing. All of that is great, but after a while you want a break. You want to go out and fill your baby lungs with some fresh air. Where I lived, the air, at this time of year, was about six degrees below zero. This sounds and is extreme, but I was unaware of what the implications of this might be. So was my sister.

I just wanted to do something different. She seemed to think it was important that I go with her, and I was ready. She bundled me up in an amazing array of sweaters and blankets. I looked less like a baby than I did Tuesday's load of wash, and I found it difficult to remain upright. My sister tied me and it all together with Mom's long scarf, stood back, and exclaimed, "Voila!" I could only roll my eyes and utter muffled baby sounds.

She topped it all off by putting Dad's joke hat on me. We called it that because he put it on when he told jokes. Poor Dad, although he was very funny, he knew only two formal jokes - the existential joke about the insurance salesman and the farmer and the one about the two, not so smart, football players from Iowa. Even at this early point in my life, I had heard these

jokes many times. They were still funny and the hat
always seemed to make them funnier.

As I sat there, I kept falling over and my sister kept
setting me back up. The hat was necessary, so that she
could tell which part of me went where.

As we made our way out the door, my sister called,
"We're going outside," to Mom, who answered ab-
sently from another room where she was involved in
rearranging furniture. My sister carried me outside
to the toboggan, which she had gotten for Christmas,
and placed me on it, saying, "We'll take the shortcut."
She sat behind me with her legs on either side to keep
me from falling off. She aimed us toward the swamp

that lay at the bottom of the great hill that was our backyard, and pushed. We were off.

The sun shone brightly as we hurtled down the hill. It was a beautiful day, and we began to travel through it at about thirty miles per hour. Snow flew into my face, and I began to laugh at the thrill of it. My sister was laughing, too. Over the sound of the wind in our ears, the rush of the snow, and the pounding of our child-like hearts we heard, quite faintly, something that sounded like our mother screaming.

We barreled forward. Together, we leaned to the right. The toboggan zipped past a tree that had threatened our progress. We threw our weight to the left, hit a little bump, and became airborne for a moment. My sister leaned forward and yelled "No brakes!" She was laughing hysterically. I'll never forget the excitement of that ride, the sense of freedom, the beauty of the winter all around us, and the feeling that nothing else existed or mattered except that moment and that hillside.

After what seemed like about two seconds, we reached the end of the hill and began to slow down.

It was then that we knew for certain that it wasn't the wind, but that Mom really was screaming. Had she wanted to go with us, I wondered? I didn't have to wait long to find out.

Mom didn't have a toboggan but she was at our side almost before we came to a stop. The first thing I noticed was that she didn't have her coat on. The next thing I knew, she was crying and hugging us. She was a little upset. I thought she seemed proud of the way we had handled the hill, but, maybe I was reading into things.

She finally collected herself and sat back on her heels to look at us. Released from her hug and unsupported, I immediately rolled to one side. She propped me against my sister and sternly asked us what we thought we were doing.

I looked up at my sister for guidance and she said, "It was his idea."

Mom started laughing. At this, I smiled through the ice on my beard and knew that everything was going to be all right.

Chapter 6

Day By Day

To me, every day was exciting. Perhaps it was because I was a baby, but I couldn't tell the difference between a day that was normal and a day that contained many momentous events.

Here's a typical day. Mom is making breakfast. Soft-boiled eggs for Dad, with a piece of dry toast on the side, and a tall glass of orange juice. My sister is eating Cheerios and coats what floats with spoonful after spoonful of sugar. She also has toast but adds lots of butter and strawberry jam. This is the difference between my father and my sister. She is trying to maximize her intake in order to grow, and he is trying to limit his in order to stay the same size.

They are both creatures of habit, and breakfast

never varies during the week. My sister is dressed for school. She is not yet fashion conscious; her socks tell you this, but she looks ready to go. My father, on the other hand, seems to be in many places at once. He isn't in a hurry, but he can't sit still. He will poke his head into the kitchen and say, "Hello, you heroes. What exciting thing is going to happen today?" We know he is talking about us, and yet we look to each other for confirmation. He then adds, "Has anyone seen my blue striped tie?" and is gone.

We continue breakfast. I, of course, perched in the high chair, am having the same old formula, but I like it. I, too, am a creature of habit. Well, creature is probably not the right word. All the same, the routine is reassuring. Each day, I try to test the limits of my ability by seeing how far I can throw the bottle. At this point, early March, I have yet to reach the table, but I am working on it.

Mom seems to have many things to do. She delivers plates to the table. She mans the toaster. Maybe I should say she Moms the toaster? Okay, she makes toast. She washes dishes in the sink. She checks the thermometer outside the window. She makes sandwiches for my sister's and my father's lunch. She reads to us from the paper - PICKUP TRUCK HEALS THE SICK, KID BLACKS OUT CITY OF 400,000 WITH SLINGSHOT, SCIENTIST TEACHES COLLIE TO TALK. She rushes out to help Dad find his pants. She rushes back to stop the tea kettle from whistling. She picks up my bottle and says, "Keep trying, Sluggo." She returns things to the refrigerator. She is nonstop and, yet, she looks peaceful and in her element.

Finally, Dad has assembled himself and returns to the kitchen. He sits down at the head of the table and surveys the heart of his domestic domain. He eyes us closely. I notice that there are only a few hairs out of place. He looks the picture of a handsome and capable Captain of Industry and, as he says to my mother, "Dear, where did you find these wonderful children?", we all smile at him with affection. Then he says seriously, "Did they come with a guarantee?"

My sister, anticipating this daily question, retorts, "Mais oui!" and pulls a long, legal-looking document from beside her. My father, equipped with legal training, examines the paper judiciously and says, "Very good. What's for breakfast?"

After my father and my sister say goodbye and disappear into the real world, my mother places me in the crib and turns on the record player. She leans back in a comfortable chair and says, "Let's take a break." The majestic notes of Rodgers and Hammerstein begin to float toward us. My mother's eyes are closed, and I close mine in imitation. As the music takes hold, this soon becomes my first nap of the day.

I wake later and find Mom doing something like knitting or reading or cleaning. I could not believe the amount of cleaning that went on in that house. Vacuuming, dusting, mopping the kitchen floor, scrubbing the tub, polishing silver, doing the laundry -- it was endless. Cleaning binges would be inter- rupted by going to the store, which was a big adventure to me, or by lunch, not such a big adventure, or by The Girls coming by.

The Girls are Mom's friends. They drop by once or twice a week. Their children are at school and, presumably, their cleaning is done. After they smile at me, poke me, tickle me, and generally get me going, talking all the while, though whether to me or to my mother I can't be certain, they sit down at the kitchen table. My mother offers them coffee and cookies. They always immediately agree to the coffee, but debate over the cookies until, finally, they decide that the cookies can do no harm. I sit in my chair and listen to their conversation. Sometimes, they play cards.

At some point in the afternoon, one of the girls discovers her watch. They all ponder the fleeting nature of

Time, for a moment, and then declare that it is time to go, that they have stayed too long, but that it has been fun so who cares, and that they will return soon. They give me the business again and depart.

Mom places me in the crib and turns the record player on. She then sits down in a comfortable chair and says, "Let's take a break." Before I know it, I am in the South Pacific. It is an enchanted evening and I am about to meet a stranger. This is the beginning of another nap.

My sister gets home from school in the mid-afternoon. Mom always asks about school, and my sister lists the important events. We learn how Miss Johnston is doing, who hit whom, who choked on paste, and who had to sit in the hall.

Dad gets home just before dinner. He says hello and disappears into his den where he mixes himself a quick cocktail, what he calls his vitamins, and looks at the paper until he gets the call for dinner from Mom.

Dinner is a time of trial for my parents. They try to reestablish contact with each other after the long day. Dad starts to tell Mom about a phone call he had in the morning, when my sister spills her milk, preempting attention. The story somehow gets lost in the mess. Or, Mom is telling Dad about something the girls told her about a mutual friend, when suddenly I toss my bottle. This leads Dad to speculate on my potential as a sports star, leaving Mom's gossip far behind in his wake.

My sister is more demanding of attention than either of my parents, and when she wants to say something, she makes sure we listen. At these moments, she clears her throat (I guess it runs in the family) and bangs her plate on the table until all eyes are on her. After she finishes, Mom looks at Dad, Dad looks at Mom, they both look at me, and then they turn toward my sister and smile weakly. By that time, my sister is on to something else entirely, like transferring peas into her mouth or lima beans into her pockets. The same thought flashes through both of my parents' minds -- soon it will be bedtime.

Bedtime is always tricky. There is no doubt that

we need our sleep and by that time of day, my sister begins to get just a bit cranky. Who can blame her? She faces a lot of frustrations. She is short, her parents are not French, she feels girls do not get equal treatment, and her brother is too small to beat up. She takes it out on her toys. I need my sleep because, although I have taken at least two naps, I am suffering from baby overload. So many new things. So much to contemplate.

My sister gets herself ready for bed by brushing her teeth, washing her face, and putting her pajamas on backwards. Being a baby, I am always ready. At bedtime, tears and laughter mix easily, but it is dark outside, there are no more meals to be had, and bed does look inviting. We might as well go to sleep. Eventually, I am in my crib and my sister is bundled in blankets in her bed.

On especially tough nights, Mom reads to us. Not from kids books, but from whatever she happens to be reading at the time. This makes for interesting dreams. One night it is Raymond Chandler.

Another, Doctor Zhivago. Once she read to us from her cookbooks. It isn't the story that is so important, it is more the sound of her voice. It speaks the magic of each word, as we release all of our own words that we have collected during the long day and drift into dreamland. In the morning, we will be well-rested and ready for another day of adventure. There is no stopping us.

Chapter 7

Dad Nears Forty

Dad had not been his usual self. His usual self said things that were funny. His usual self was energetic. His usual self did not complain, and he had been complaining lately. He said things like, "I'm just an old fart", or "I better enjoy this hair while I've got it", or pointing toward his stomach, "What is this thing?"

One day, my sister asked Mom, "What's an old fart?" Dad was down in his den.

Mom ignored the question and said, "Children, at your age, it may be hard to understand, but growing up can be difficult."

My sister and I looked at each other. We understood more than she knew.

"Your father is getting near his fortieth birthday. In fact, it's next week and a fortieth birthday is a kind of milestone. At forty, you've reached a mature age which means that, if you can face the facts, you can see that your youth is gone. This isn't a bad thing. It is just the way life is. You find yourself at a different stage of life with a different perspective, one that is deeper, richer, and more rewarding."

She was losing us here.

"Your father is beginning to realize that life is finite, that his body is deteriorating, and that you can't turn back the hands of Time. This may sound depressing, but there is another side to it. Those first forty years have their own wonderful life. You can look at those first forty years as a time of training, a time of organization, a preparation for a time when you can fully understand and appreciate the beauty of life. You are able to understand it as a precious gift that should not be taken for granted."

We were both beginning to yawn. Mom was looking off into the distance, as if she was actually seeing the future in all its varied detail.

"When you are young, you think you are going to live forever."

This woke us up.

My sister asked for both of us, "We're not?"

"It just seems that way. You think that there is all the time in the world to accomplish your dreams, but dreams require planning and hard work. There are endless distractions, and it takes a lot of effort to figure out what is important. All the while, Time rolls on. Despite life's finite nature, the paradox is that in each moment there exists a lifetime and with attention and honesty and love, Time doesn't matter."

That was all very well, but we were still concerned about living forever. Mom reassured us that we had long lives ahead of us. They would be longer and more interesting than we could possibly imagine, and we would always have her love. We were willing to let this question go, for the moment.

My sister then asked, "But what about Dad?"

"Well, your father is a little worried. Although not

a particularly vain man, your father is a man, and all men, though they pretend otherwise, are vain. As we age, our bodies change. Each year you grow taller, muscles develop, coordination increases."

She now looked at me.

"And, for men, a sign that they are maturing is that they begin to grow beards. Your brother, here, is an exceptional baby. But around age forty, without close attention and even with it, your body begins to deteriorate physically. This is what is distressing your father.

"That small and endearing bulge around his middle is just part of this whole thing. The other part is that people make a big deal of turning forty because it makes them nervous. For some, it should make them nervous and will hopefully refocus them on the important things in life.

"Your father is a wonderful, intelligent, and sensitive man. He has two wonderful children and a wife who loves him. He has work that satisfies him, most of the time, and he has close friends. That's enough for anyone. He sees that, and it is because of all these good things that he is worried. He doesn't want to lose them. He knows he can't hold onto them forever; he can only enjoy them and give to them and help them. But even though he knows all this, it is hard to accept, and so he sometimes focuses on the smaller details of growing older."

My sister and I then thought of those smaller details -- his graying hair, his endearing bulge, his aching back, his advancing age -- and we decided we loved all of those things, although we, ourselves, were determined to never turn forty.

"What your father knows and will soon admit is that his fortieth birthday is only one day. It is just a signal. We'll still have breakfast the next day. No birthday can change that. It will still be his life, and we will all still be in it. And he will be grateful that he is alive and will know that while one is alive, all things are possible."

She then looked fondly at us and said, "I'm so glad we are all together," and hugged us.

We looked at Mom.

My sister spoke the unspoken question, "What about you? Will you be ever be forty?"

Mom smiled serenely at us and said, "You don't have to worry about me. When my time comes, I will always remain thirty-nine."

Chapter 8

The Blizzard

Minnesota is called the Land of Ten Thousand Lakes. That sounds so beautiful. What they don't tell you is that most of them are frozen. Or frozen for six or seven months of the year. If you are born there, like we were, you get used to it and eventually come to be filled with a perverse sense of defiance. My father had it bad. The challenge that below-zero weather gave my father was unlike any other. The car could freeze, the pipes could freeze, your ears could freeze, turn brown, and fall off, and yet there he would be, outside of his warm house, every day, in the cold, defying the elements.

As he scraped the ice from the windshield of the car, he would be laughing at the cold and daring it to be colder. He would examine the drifts of snow and disdainfully wonder if that was the best Nature could do. The more severe the weather was, the more he liked it, the more exciting he found it, and the more he tried to prove his independence from it. That's why the blizzard we had was so amazing. It took a very big storm to make him lay low.

It started one night after dinner. During the time between dinner and bedtime, Dad peeked out the window and saw that it was beginning to snow. He reported this to us. There was no alarm in his voice. This was a normal occurrence in the winter. My sister, as a matter of form, asked if she would have to go to school the next day.

My father laughed and said, "No little bit of snow is going to keep us home."

Although my sister liked school, she found the idea of being excused from it thrilling, whether because of holiday, snow, or sickness. But she tried to be like my father in her defiance of Nature and said, "Yeah, let it snow a foot. Who cares?" and laughed dramatically.

I had little interest in whether it snowed or not. I wasn't going anywhere.

The wonder of snow soon faded during the more immediate battle of bedtime. But when my sister and I were finally settled in the darkness and quiet before sleep, we listened to the wind rattle the windows and to the snow, which was being driven before it, and began to wonder some more.

When we woke the next morning, we knew something was different. The wind was howling and the radio was on. Mom was listening to the weather. Reports from tiny towns out on the plains or from up North were given -- drifting and blowing snow, 18 to 20 inches, 40-mile-per-hour winds, windchill temperatures in the minus thirties, roads impassable. Not encouraging for motorists. The local report was similar, and this was easy to confirm. We just looked out the window. We couldn't see across the driveway.

Mom checked the thermometer. Minus 10 degrees. The list of school closings was being read on the radio. I wondered how there could be that many schools. And all those kids? There must be millions of them. Up to this point, I just assumed that there was me and my sister and the kids in her school. This news was something to think about.

My sister had her ear almost on the speaker of the radio. She was waiting to hear the name of her school. She waited and waited.

She said to my mother, "They don't even know we exist."

Mom was making toast.

My father came in and said to my sister, "Don't even bother. We'll just get in the car and fishtail all the way to school."

My mother groaned.

"But, Dad," my sister said, "we could get stuck and freeze to death. They'd dig us out next spring and there we'd be, in the front seat, staring forward and listening to the radio."

My sister had a vivid imagination.

"They'd be playing Hound Dog and my lunch would still be good, except that it would be frozen, and I would have missed all the fun stuff at school and Mom would be waiting for us and I'd never get to Paris then, because I'd be dead."

My sister started crying at this point, and Mom looked sternly at my father, who raised his eyebrows at me and began to dismiss the storm which was still raging outside. He told of how it had been when he had been a boy and how they didn't even have cars then. If they had a storm like this, they had to put their snowshoes on and put hot rocks into their pockets to keep themselves warm and walk to school, which was six or seven miles from their old homestead. He said they would scatter breadcrumbs behind them as they went, so that they would be able to find their way home.

No one was listening to him, except me, and I imagined Dad slogging through the drifts in his coonskin hat and mittens. He was leaning forward at an absurd angle and was laughing as the wind and snow tried to drive him backwards.

Dad went on to describe how he and the other

children arrived at the schoolhouse, which was six or seven miles from anywhere else, and found that only the peak of the roof was showing above the deep snow. They used their snowshoes to dig out their school.

As they cleared the snow away from the door, their teacher, the beautiful Miss Pearson, emerged and said to them, "Hurry up, the bell is about to ring."

Nothing had stopped them back then, my father said, and this little storm wouldn't stop us now.

The reports on the radio became even more serious. The announcer was advising everyone to stay home and reporting that the end of the storm was nowhere in sight. They even announced the name of my sister's school. She was very relieved and double-checked with Mom to make sure that she wouldn't have to go.

My father was quieting down now and was listening, too. He got up and studied the scene outside the window. There wasn't much to study. Snow was blowing almost horizontally and was so thick you couldn't see anything.

At this point, it was either time to leave for work or time to return to bed. My father considered himself responsible for all of the others at his office and decided he would go to work.

He said, "Gotta go. See you later. I'll call you when I get to work."

Mom looked at him with concern, but knew he would do whatever he had decided.

My sister pleaded with him to stay, crying that he might be in a wreck, we would never see him again, his ears would fall off.

He looked seriously at her and said, "Kiddo, thanks for the concern, but don't worry." He began to puff himself up and said, "You know, I laugh at the snow and it's going to take more of a storm than this to keep me from my appointed rounds. Neither sleet, snow, rain, mud, potholes, or anything else can stop me. I won't have it."

With that, he flung his scarf over his shoulder with a flourish and, with a devilish laugh, was gone.

It was snowing so hard, we never saw him go.

We just heard the rumble of the car's engine briefly beneath the roar of the storm. My sister asked if this had anything to do with Dad turning forty. Mom didn't answer. She was looking out the window, and on her face was an expression of worry.

It became a very quiet house except for the radio, which droned on with the names of obscure school districts and now the names of businesses that had closed. We each thought about Dad and imagined him in danger out there, laughing bravely at the snow. As the minutes passed slowly, our thoughts became gloomier. We heard the name of Dad's business broadcast on the radio. His office was closed, and yet, he was deep in the snow fighting each step of the way to get there. I wondered if his ears would really fall off.

At that moment, there was a pounding on the front door. We all jumped a foot. Was this a telegram about Dad? The troopers returning his frozen shell? Mom leaped up and went to the door. She threw it open. There was a huge cloud of snow and a blast of cold air, and through it stepped Dad. He was still laughing.

"Well," he said, somewhat embarrassed, "I couldn't get to the end of the driveway, and I realized I would rather spend the day here with you, where my ears won't fall off, than anywhere else. Let's get out the toboggan."

My mother threw her arms around my father, in spite of the snow on him, and said, "No toboggan."

Chapter 9

Mom Meets Dad

One day, my sister, who, for some reason, was interested in these things, asked Mom how she and Dad had met. It was afternoon, and we were lying around. Mom was reading, my sister was drawing, and I was staring out into space. We had a little time before dinner, so Mom, who had at first blushed and then smiled broadly, said, "Ok, here's the story."

"When I was a young woman, about twenty years old and at college, the great thing to do in the summer was to go to the beach. Everyone used to go. You wouldn't believe how many kids turned out. There were volleyball games in the sand, people were swimming and splashing around, some were tanning, some reading, and everyone was glad to be outside and near the water. There were groups of us girls who would sit together and talk about everything -- politics, weather, each other, our figures, but we especially liked to talk about men. Or boys, as we called them.

"There were also groups of boys, though they probably thought of themselves as men, and they also were talking among themselves. It's hard for me to imagine what they were talking about, but, at that time, we hoped it might be about us. We didn't know anything about men. For all we knew, they were talking about their cars or of something unsavory or about philosophy.

"We all ate hot dogs and chips and soft drinks and talked and thought about the future out there under the sun. We sat around like this all day, every day. But at night, everything was different. The lights at the beach were dim and were swallowed up by the darkness and by the great expanse of water and sand. We built huge fires of driftwood. Half-lit by the fires or half-lit by the moon and the stars, the beach, with its soft sand and constant song of the waves, became a world of romance.

"The separate groups of girls and boys, who were shy by day, became a bolder, more friendly crowd by night. There were young fellows there with guitars, and we all sang together. We cooked more hot dogs. Boys and girls talked to each other, and some fell in love.

"I was interested in the boys, but I wasn't particularly interested in falling in love. I had school to think of, and there were many things I wanted to do. Plus, I had seen many movies and had read quite a bit by this time, and knew that there was a lot of heartache in the world.

"Well, one night I was standing by the campfire with my friend, Miriam, who was a nice girl and a gorgeous blonde to boot. We were singing the words to a popular song. I can't remember the name of it, but it was very sentimental. I looked across the fire and around at the circle of faces singing and I noticed a young man staring right at us. He was very bold.

I thought, at first, that he was looking at Miriam. After all, she was the blonde. But no, he was looking at me. Before I looked away, I saw that he was tall and quite handsome, with dark hair. He was smiling.

"I looked up again and he was gone. I was so disappointed. I looked at Miriam to see if she had noticed, but she was still singing. The next thing I knew, someone tapped me on the shoulder. I turned and looked. No one was there. I felt a tap on my other shoulder. I turned and there was your father, the boy from the other side of the fire. He wasn't your father then. I had never seen him before. He was laughing and I told him that his little trick was really stupid. He said, 'Yeah, I know.'

"Well, we got to talking, and it turned out that he was very nice. He had good manners and was really funny. It wasn't that he told jokes; he just had a sense of humor. He did tell one joke. He said it was an existential joke. It was the same one you've heard about the insurance salesman and the farmer, and I didn't think it was that funny, even then. But he was also serious and seemed very sweet. We talked about what we were studying at school, and he told me he was studying business.

"We went for a walk along the beach and talked for hours. When it was time for me to go home, he walked me back to where the crowd was and as we got closer, he began acting a little strange. Then he suddenly leaned over and kissed me. It was totally unannounced and unexpected, and I slapped him. I liked him, but it was a reflex. As soon as I slapped him, his face went white and he turned and threw up. It was the most amazing thing. At first, I thought it was because of all the hot dogs, but it turned out that he was in love with me.

"He was so embarrassed. I apologized and tried to reassure him that it was all right and that, in spite of what happened, I liked him, too, but he felt terrible. He gathered his dignity together and said that he was sorry he had kissed me. He said he realized that he had made a fool of himself. He looked me in the eye, said goodnight, and walked off.

"I went to find Miriam. She asked me where I had been, but I didn't know what to tell her. When I did tell her, she thought I was kidding. I discovered, by telling her about the whole thing, that even though he had thrown up, I really did like him.

"We went back to the beach every night. I looked for his face around the fire, but I never saw him. We sang the songs and had fun, but I kept looking for him. I wanted to tell him that everything was ok. I wanted to tell him something. Miriam thought I was crazy. One night, it was getting late and Miriam wanted to go home, but I persuaded her to stay for one more song. As I sang, I thought of how afraid we all are of each other and how big and lonely the world can be.

"I was looking at the fire, and I was thinking that it was almost the end of the summer, when I felt a tap on my shoulder. I turned and no one was there. I turned around the other way and there he was. He saw that I was glad to see him. He blushed and looked down at his feet and said, 'Hi'."

My mother stopped then, and everything was quiet. My sister and I looked at each other. We didn't know quite how to take this story.

My sister said weakly, "Wow."

I mumbled something and looked thoughtfully into the distance. Mom was smiling. She sighed, deeply, and got up to make dinner.

Chapter 10

Mom's Strange Idea

My mother was a very curious person. One way she exhibited this was to read anything and everything she could get her hands on. As a result, she had some strange ideas.

While she was waiting to have me, she had been reading a book about African explorers. In this book, there was a section on Mary Kingsley, a Victorian Englishwoman, who had spent a lot of time in the swamps of Africa. It told how she had encountered a tribe who carried their children everywhere. In fact, the children were not allowed to touch the ground until they were three years old.

My mother was intrigued by this idea. It was supposed to convey, to the child, the support and concern of the parents. Once assured by three years of this, by no means a short period of time to a child, the children, no longer babies, were set loose in the world.

My mother made a decision and had every intention of following this procedure with me, her second born. Her firstborn, my sister, had in her opinion not turned out badly, but knowledge is power, and there was always room for improvement. Before I was born, she had rigged up a crude contraption that would hold me on her back wherever she might go. In addition to this, there was what had formerly been my sister's high chair and a crib whose sleeping surface was, I thought once I was in it, a long way from the ground.

My father, who was used to this kind of thing, encouraged her by saying, "Why three years? Why not six or seven?" He made helpful suggestions, such as, "Hey, we could leave him in the car the whole time," or "I can take him with me when I play golf. I'll just get another caddie."

Mom paid no attention to him but became more determined. Unfortunately, there had been no scientific studies on this type of child-rearing. Dr. Spock did not mention it in his book. No one else that Mom knew of had done this sort of thing before, and she considered herself a pioneer.

When I came along and presented myself to her and my father as a somewhat different baby, it really threw her. The fact of my beard she took as a sign that perhaps she should reconsider her somewhat unorthodox plans. Maybe I was already different enough, and her plan might complicate my possibly uncertain future. Also, a vision of carrying a bearded bundle on her back was at odds with the picture she had been forming of our first three years together.

My mother, however, had a stubborn streak in her which made itself known from time to time. This was one of those times, and so she carried me everywhere. I was carried from the hospital to the car. From the car to the couch. From the couch to the crib and from the crib to my high chair. It was a good thing I was not afraid of heights. She carried me to my grandparents' house. She carried me home.

As time went on, I began to look down at my legs and my feet and my toes and wonder why I couldn't use them as I saw my sister and my parents doing. In frustration and defiance, I placed my toes in my mouth and, to my surprise, found the sensation tasty and pleasurable. If I was to be denied their use, I would, at least, take sustenance and solace from them.

Mom might carry me everywhere, but each time she set me down, I would immediately go to work on my toes. I have to admit that part of this behavior was because I could see it bothered her. Between the good taste and the idea of rebellion, I was incited to pursue this activity almost all of my waking hours.

My sister would walk by and say, in a sneering and superior way, "Ish," and sometimes she stopped and lectured me on hygiene. She would ask, "Do you know where those feet have been?" I looked up at her feigning ignorance and she would continue, "If you keep doing that, your toes will be so long they won't fit into your shoes and your teeth will stick out." At that time, I didn't have shoes or teeth, and this made little impression on me.

My sister knew a thing or two and, after a while, she came over and said, "You can't fool me. You're trying to drive Mom crazy, so she'll let you out."

I looked up at her with affection. She knew, she understood. She didn't want me imprisoned, deprived of movement and mobility. She wanted to be able to play with me. I could feel that she disliked the separation between us that my restriction forced on her.

She looked around and then whispered, "It's working. Keep it up."

My father let all this go on for about a month, and then he saw that my mother was beginning to have doubts about the value of her plan. He knew she was stubborn and would have a hard time admitting that this might not be such a good idea. He saw my eagerness to get out and about and had understood the dual nature of my attraction to my toes.

One night, as they looked down at me performing this act, he said, "I'm no expert, but won't that affect his feet? They may become abnormally long. And do you think all that sucking will affect his smile?"

Mom said nothing, but, later, she found it hard to sleep.

He began to suggest that this obsession of mine was affecting me in many ways. "Have you noticed he isn't talking much?" (Not that I could) or "He seems more interested in those toes than he is in his bottle." The one that finally got her was when he said, "He's so curled up, I'm afraid he may never unravel." She had replied, "Oh, go on," but we all noticed that she was seriously shaken about the whole situation.

On a Friday night, not long after this, she gathered us together in the living room. It was obvious she had an announcement to make. She looked at each of us, took a deep breath, and said, "Sometimes you get possessed by an idea that no one else understands. Everyone may think you are crazy, but that doesn't mean that you are necessarily wrong. It doesn't mean you should forget it. It's important to find out for yourself what the story really is. But if it turns out that you are wrong, you should never be afraid to admit it and change your mind."

My sister said, "Amen."

Mom went on, "I realize that by following this idea of mine, I have kept one of us from developing on his own, and I have kept all of us from becoming even closer than we are. I know now that I was mistaken, and I apologize to all of you."

She then came over to me and said, "Especially to you."

She picked me up, gave me a quick hug, and placed me on the carpet. It was the greatest feeling, seeing that beige ocean extend all the way to the far walls and knowing that I could go anywhere my little arms and legs could take me. I wiggled my toes with excitement. I closed my eyes in joy.

When I opened them, I saw that my mother, my father, and my sister were there on the floor with me. We all began crawling around and giggling.

My mother was trying her best to put her toes in her mouth and asked me, "Are they really that good?"

Chapter 11

Baby Solidarity

One day, the neighbors came to visit. Not all the neighbors. That would have been ridiculous. The family that lived closest to us, had, all by itself, five children and a mother and a father, and that's seven. It was the mother of this closest neighboring family and her youngest who came to visit. Her youngest was a baby like me. Well, not exactly like me.

They came over one afternoon, and my mother welcomed them at the door. This other mother was not one of The Girls, but she was a good friend of my mother's. I noticed as she came in that she was carrying her baby. I hoped that this didn't mean she and Mom had been talking. I hated to think of another baby being deprived of his freedom. It didn't appear that she had been unduly influenced, because she plopped her baby down in the middle of the living room floor, right next to where I was resting on my blanket.

The neighboring mother had already heard about my beard from Mom, so only a quick flicker in her appraising gaze gave away her slight shock. She looked me over, and I reciprocated. She was more motherly looking, I thought, than my mother. Maybe it was because she was heavier and there was just more of her motherliness. Her hair was blonde, and her blue eyes looked like they knew how to laugh. I liked her. Especially, when she said, "He's so distinguished looking and so handsome."

I blushed.

Then, she said, "He looks like a handful."

My mother laughed and said, "Yes, we have to keep him tied up most of the day."

In distress, I looked at her, but saw that she was kidding. I didn't think this was so funny and turned away

from these adults and confronted the neighbor who
was my own age.

He was small and possessed some wispy light brown
hair that seemed like it wasn't sure just where to take
root on his head. His hands and feet were quite pudgy,
and his general shape was round. He had a friendly
and trusting face, and his eyes were like his mother's.

He had no beard, but I wasn't expecting him to. At
this point, I knew that I was unusual, some might
say odd, but this did not disturb me. I wasn't really
aware of what it might mean or what problems this
beard might cause me in the future. It didn't make
me unbearably proud, and I didn't feel superior to

other babies. I just liked having a beard. It would heat up in the sunshine and it kept me warm at night. It had a wonderful color and gave shape to my otherwise slightly unformed head. I enjoyed it and simply thought of it as part of the package.

My young neighbor crawled over and we looked at each other. I knew somehow that he was going to pull on my beard, and so I was prepared for it, but I was surprised by the ferocity of the tug. I think he was, too. I let out a squeal of protest, as if to say, "All right, already."

I knew he only wanted to prove its authenticity to himself, and I approved. You can't always take your mother's word for things. Once satisfied, we began to wrestle. We rolled on the blanket and over each other. We made fierce noises and faces at each other, but they were only for show. Every now and then, we would take a break and lie on the blanket, looking at each other and panting from exertion.

It was good to play with someone the same age and size. I couldn't wrestle with my sister. She would kill me. My young neighbor and I seemed to have the same outlook on life -- fresh and innocent. We looked the world in the eye from ground level, and were excited by what we saw.

Our mothers, from time to time, looked down from their coffee, startled by our noise. When they saw that no ears were missing and that we seemed to be having a good time, they went back to their conversation.

My sister, at one point, cruised through the room, saw us playing on the floor, and said haughtily, "Babies, will they ever grow up?"

As the afternoon went on, my neighbor and I realized that a baby didn't have to be lonely. We were a part of a whole wave of babies, and babies could support each other and visit and compare notes. They could gnaw on each other's legs and experiment with facial expressions. They could help each other in ways we were just beginning to discover, and they could look twice as cute when they were together. We couldn't foresee the result of all these babies, but we reveled in the fact that we were not alone, that others of our kind existed. With a new confidence, we went back to wrestling and making wild noises.

It became time for our neighbors to go home and the two mothers got up and were saying goodbye-sounding things to each other. Of course, the babies had not been consulted in this, and so we ignored them and continued playing. All of a sudden, our mothers swooped down and plucked us from the floor and from each other. We were not to be so easily parted.

We cried, we screamed, we howled. Our mothers were not prepared for this. It even surprised us. After it became apparent that we were not going to stop anytime soon, they put us back on the blanket that was our playground. We were immediately at peace. We knew it was time to go, but we wanted to say goodbye in our own way.

We looked at each other and, though no words were spoken, we knew that more than a wrestling match had taken place. As our mothers watched, my neighbor crawled over and gave my beard a playful tug. I made a face at him that made him laugh so hard, he fell over. We weren't yet able to walk, but I knew we had just taken the first steps of friendship.

Chapter 12

Be Your Own Boss

My sister was very mature for her age. By this I don't mean she was six feet tall. I mean she knew things. She knew Geography and proved it by teaching me the capitals of all the states. She knew the difference between a Ford and a Chevy. She had developed her powers of observation to a point where it seemed as if she could read my mind. "Don't look at me that way," she would say. I would think, "What way?" and then, upon reflection, realize that I had been thinking that her barrette was really in bad taste.

She had acquired a surprising command of the French language and all things French. She would exclaim, "Mon Dieu!" and was very fond of French fries.

She shocked my mother by suggesting, one night, that perhaps at some time in the future we could have frog legs for dinner. Her favorite painters were Edouard Manet and Henri Rousseau, though it may have had something to do with how their names sounded.

She was quite self-possessed and didn't lose her temper or cry much, preferring to adopt a somewhat distant and worldly stance toward the normal trials and tribulations of growing up. She was unlike her friends and classmates in this. They would be fighting over a doll, with earnest tears, and she would look at them and comment on the impermanence of childhood. I've seen her do it. I don't mean to suggest that she was cold or inhuman, but just that she had the ability to see things from another perspective.

She had a reservoir of ambition that seemed unique in our family. Her plans for guiding the future of the French state were an example of this. It seemed like she studied all the time. She not only had her nose in a book, it seemed she would crawl right into it entirely. Once she read about leopards and painted spots all over herself and didn't speak or get off of all fours for two days. Mom and Dad tried to reason with her, but she arched her back, hissed threateningly, and took a swipe at them with her paw.

Another example of her unbounded ambition was the mail she received. One day, she started getting stuff in the mail. At first, Mom thought it was some kind of mix-up, but it kept coming. Every few days my sister would receive, addressed to her, a pamphlet which would announce in bold letters - EARN $$$ AT HOME IN YOUR SPARE TIME. BE YOUR OWN BOSS!. It would go on to explain how, by stuffing envelopes or something, my sister would soon have enough money to buy a new car.

She was sent information on how to become a locksmith. How to start your own import business. Sharpen lawn mower blades. Start a saw mill. Study interior design. Mechanical drafting. It was end-less. Home correspondence school material lined the shelves of our bedroom. She was learning the secrets of the Rosicrucians. She was becoming a veterinarian.

My father thought my sister was a budding businessman and entrepreneur like himself. Mom didn't know what to think. Her daughter a sawmill operator? She finally put her foot down when she saw, among the innocent looking bills, a piece of literature with a headline that blared - DEVELOP A BEAUTIFUL BUST IN ONLY ONE MINUTE A DAY. This was not her idea of the kind of material my sister should possess.

My sister did know the value of a dollar. She would save every cent she could get her hands on. Her eyes were always on the ground, looking for that fumbled penny or that displaced dime. She would do extra chores to add to her horde of coins. She even participated in what, I thought, was a ghoulish practice -- selling her teeth.

Maybe it was because I didn't have any teeth. Maybe I just had no understanding and appreciation of tradition. Maybe I wasn't mature enough, but the idea of selling a part of your body, especially one that had been in your mouth, to someone you didn't even know, was one I couldn't grasp. And to a mysterious, super-natural being at that.

What did this Tooth Fairy want them for? What did the Tooth Fairy do with them? I couldn't imagine it, and when my sister told me that the Tooth Fairy takes them from all the kids, I was really concerned. What if you didn't want to give them up? Would he come down one night and extract them?

As I lay in my crib, thinking about this, I had my first misgivings about growing up. It shook me. It also unnerved me to see the lengths to which my sister would go to get the Fairy's dime or quarter. As I watched her, I began to have an inkling of the concept and power of greed.

She leaned over the edge of my crib many times, in the days preceding this event, and bared her teeth at me. She made unintelligible sounds while pointing to one of her incisors. She then grabbed it and began wiggling it just inches from my face. I tried to assume an expression of interest and sympathy, but what I really felt was bewilderment. Why would she do this?

It seemed that she was forcing the issue.

Finally, after days of this, came the big showdown. As I watched, and I am not making this up, she attached one end of a piece of string to the doorknob and the other end to her tooth. I saw what she meant to do. She pulled the door toward her, in readiness. She looked at me for support, and my heart went out to her. Her face, at that moment, was not the face of a mature, mercenary child. It was the face of a scared kid with a toothache.

She let the door slam and gave a shriek. She had been successful on the first try. Evidently, she had learned something from all those mailings. She picked up the tooth and rushed over to me. She was a sight. In her hand she held the tooth, which was interesting but not very attractive, and she smiled widely so that I could see the place it had come from. There was now a small gap between the other teeth with a little blood flowing from it. She was glowing with triumph.

Alerted by my sister's shriek, my parents had joined

us. They congratulated and comforted her. My father looked at me and raised his eyebrows as if to say, "Can you believe it?"

He then said, "This could happen to you."

I gave a start and shook my head.

When things settled down, my parents got me and my sister to bed. They tucked my sister in and assured her that the Tooth Fairy would come that night and take her tooth and leave her money. My sister, needless to say, was excited. She was to put the tooth under her pillow, and when she woke up, she would find what the Fairy had left.

When our parents were gone, she told me that she wanted to wait up for the Tooth Fairy and negotiate. I didn't think this was a good idea, but I was very curious about him. I decided that I would stay awake that night and although I wasn't about to help her negotiate, I wanted to see what he looked like and discover how well he could bargain with my sister.

Despite her plan to wait up, my sister, exhausted by the ordeal of losing her tooth, was asleep in about three minutes. I stayed up. I waited and waited. The moon moved across the window. The house was silent. And dark.

I thought about my sister. She had been motivated by money and momentum and guided by her childlike maturity, yet what really stood out in my mind had been that moment of truth before she had slammed the door. She didn't have to do that. The tooth would have fallen out on its own, but she had wanted to be the boss in her own life and had, I saw now, bravely gone ahead. I thought she was great. I hoped he left her a dollar.

The clock ticked on. My eyes were getting heavy, but I felt that he would be there any minute. I yawned. I tried to focus on the door of the bedroom. He probably had a lot of stops that night. I yawned again. The clock ticked on and on and, as I listened to it, time slowed down. The ticking became fainter and fainter, as I strained to hear it. I took a deep breath and was asleep.

Chapter 13

Dad Works Out

We were basically a healthy family. We ate well, we got plenty of sleep, and, if not exactly exercise fanatics, we were at least an active family. My father sat behind a desk a lot at work and he sat in his den a lot at home, but even he shoveled snow. Also, each week without fail, he did his exercises after he got up on Saturday morning. I watched him sometimes.

He began by assuming a pained look on his face and then reached toward the ceiling, first with one arm and then with the other. He made exercise noises while he did this. Grunting with effort. He then bent forward and attempted to touch his toes. Those toes were farther away from his fingers than they should have been, but it seems some people's legs are just longer than their arms.

Sometimes his aching back would decide to pay my father back for various moments of abuse and neglect and would freeze at the most downward position of his toe touching. When this happened, my father would really make some noises. Noises in earnest. Noises that might, by their very urgency and sincerity, ease his back muscles into a relaxed state. There were short staccato bursts of "Oh, oh, oh," and "ah, ah, ah, ah," punctuated by a pained intake of breath. No one could stay in such a position for very long and, after a few moments, my father's back would relent.

Most men would take this as a sign to go slow, to either proceed more gently with the exercises or to abandon them altogether. Not my Dad. To him, it was a call to redouble his efforts and to blast through the obstructions in his path. He didn't see it as a knot, where the harder you pulled, the tighter it got. He saw it as if it were a jar that wouldn't open, and if you banged it enough on its edge and applied an adrenaline assisted rush of effort, your will would triumph over the inherent obstinacy of objects. His zeal was admirable, if not wise. He would do one more toe touch to establish his authority and then move on to the other exercises.

It was a good thing we had our own house, because if we had had downstairs neighbors when my father did jumping jacks, everyone would have been upset. As it was, my sister rushed into my parents' bedroom wondering if the house were about to fall down. When she saw that it was only Dad, she sat down on the bed and, in silence, watched him.

Dad was chugging away and chanting, "One, two, three..." etc. His hands came together over his head as his feet shot out toward the walls. He looked at my sister, out of the corner of his eye, in between movements. It seemed she made him nervous.

He said, "Care to join me?"

My sister, in a cheeky mood, said, "Dahling, but of course," and took her place facing him.

They chanted in unison, "Sixteen, seventeen,

eighteen..." They were smiling and were beginning to sweat.

Mom stuck her head in and nodded in time to the counting and then chuckled to herself as she returned to her chores. Around thirty-one, my sister began to wonder how many Dad was going to do. At forty-one, she dropped out of formation and excused herself, saying that Mom needed her in the kitchen. This was all right with Dad, as he was moving on to the more difficult exercises, and he was not inclined to have his daughter see him struggle.

Panting, he lowered himself to the floor and placed his legs straight out in front of him. This next exercise was a variation of the toe touching, but from a sitting position. One might think that having all important parts on ground level would facilitate the attempt, but one would be wrong. Though paradoxical, it seemed the toes were even farther away than before. In his favor, it must be said that my father made the effort. At least three times.

He then abandoned this and went on to the important and somewhat easier sit-ups. Here the grunting got serious. Were his stomach muscles weak, or was it that the thoughts in his head were so weighty? Dad had a problem with sit-ups. After about twelve of them, the smooth action of his muscles was gone. In a quick and what might be seen as a desperate effort, Dad would jerk himself up to a sitting position.

He had a goal, and he was pursuing it. The numbers increased with each jerk and with each jerk his body was somehow propelled backwards toward the wall. It was only an inch or so with each situp, but by number forty-eight, only two away from his goal of fifty, he hit his head on the baseboard. Slightly dazed, he scrunched himself forward and completed the remaining two.

As he lay on his back, chest heaving, it struck him that exercise is a lonely thing. Every Saturday, there on the floor, he competed against no one but himself. A test of Will, and his will, at the moment, was beginning to weaken. He wondered, but only for a moment, whether he ought to go help my mother in the kitchen. Then he laughed weakly and, with an effort, pushed the thought from his mind.

He concentrated on his next assignment -- leg lifts. His body went rigid as his heels came unsteadily off the carpet, until they were several inches off the floor. The longer they hovered there, the faster he counted and soon, with a thump, they returned. I could see he had had enough of that, and he rolled over for push-ups.

His arms proved stronger than his stomach, and the push-ups proceeded in an orderly fashion. As he lowered himself toward the floor, he tried to see how close to the carpet he could bring his nose. He thought of it as adding to the challenge. It did. It made his eyes cross. He worried about smashing his nose. He began to lose count. It was just as well; he was tired. He lowered himself to the floor and caught his breath.

His last exercise was a stretching position borrowed from yoga called The Cobra. This was meant to both strengthen and loosen the spine. It began with my father lying on his stomach. He placed his hands on either side of his shoulders and pushed up, leaving his legs relaxed on the floor and arching his neck and spine backwards toward them.

My sister and mother were in the kitchen when they heard Dad's agonized cry. They ran to the door of the bedroom and looked down on him. He was arched backwards, and his face was contorted in pain. His back had frozen once more. He couldn't go up, and he couldn't go down. They knelt beside him and asked what they could do. Dad was breathing raggedly and couldn't talk.

My sister said she had heard somewhere that walking on the back helped it and offered her services.

Dad managed a quick, authoritative, and frightened, "No."

They, then, both began to gently massage his back. It seemed to be working. His breathing came more smoothly, and, after a moment, he was able to slowly lower himself to the comfort of the carpet.

At last, he was completely horizontal. His head was turned to one side, and he breathed his grateful thanks to Mom and my sister.

My mother looked at him and said, "Champ, listen. We're proud of the fact that you're here on the floor trying your best, but take it easy. You don't have to hurt yourself. There's always time to get in shape."

Chapter 14

The New Do

My mother was not a slave of fashion. She wore clothes and she looked nice, but she didn't have a consuming interest in them. She talked clothes sometimes with The Girls, but they then moved on to other things like food or children. We didn't have beauty and fashion magazines around the house; we had *National Geographic, Fortune, Time, and Life*. As a family, life was more important than fashion. We liked Mom just the way she was.

She didn't wear a lot of makeup and didn't spend hours on her nails. She had better things to do, like trying to take care of us. However, she did like to get her hair done. It was her one indulgence. She would go to the beauty shop every two weeks.

I don't know what it was about it that she liked so much. Having someone work on your hair seemed more like a bother than a pleasure to me. Perhaps it just felt good to her -- someone shampooing, combing, and styling her hair. Maybe it was just the idea of someone doing something for her. After all, she was always doing something for us, and we really didn't help her much. We ate all the good meals and then messed up the house.

Whatever the reason, she went to the beauty shop regularly. I heard about it from my sister who, many times, had been there with her. My sister said it didn't look like much from the outside, but inside it was really something. There were sinks all over the place. There were lots of chairs and some that swiveled around in circles. There were huge, electric machines, like toasters, under which the women sat when they were drying their hair. There were also magazines, thousands of them, and all concerning fashion.

My sister, at this time, did not share Mom's enthusiasm for all this. Although she did find the magazines entertaining, funny she said, she found that waiting for Mom and her hair was really boring. The other thing she didn't like about it was the smell. According to her, the beauty shop had an odor about it that she found herself at a loss to describe. The closest she ever came was to say that it was not the smell of something edible and that it was not the smell of something you would want to carry around on the top of your head.

My sister went on to tell me that only ladies went there and that some of them looked like they had never left. Their hair had even turned color. Not from brown to blonde, as so many women were doing, but from whatever color it had originally been to blue or to some other completely unnatural shade.

We couldn't understand this power that the beauty shop had over women, and we were worried that our mother might get carried away. We definitely did not want a mom with blue hair. Once, my sister begged her not to go, and Mom looked at her with concern, but without comprehension.

Mom had no intention of becoming a blonde or a

blue or anything else. She went there regularly and returned the same day, looking very much her usual self but with hair that seemed to have more spring and more shine. Not altogether a bad thing. And, best of all, Mom really enjoyed these visits.

My father, although he always commented on her hair after these trips to the beauty shop, really didn't seem too interested. He was glad she enjoyed herself and everything, but he didn't really understand what all the fuss was about. He liked her just the way she was. He thought that she always looked great. We did, too.

One week, my mother went for her appointment, and she didn't take my sister. We didn't think anything about it. She would simply return at some point and then start to make dinner. But this time things were different.

She came back about four o'clock and she had a new hairdo. Right away we could see that Mom had either been looking at the magazines or had taken the styling advice of someone new. We barely recognized her.

My sister and I looked at each other uncertainly and thought, "Mom?" It was a real shocker.

For one thing, Mom's hair had always been shoulder length. It hung down in waves, and she brushed it back to one side, sometimes pinning it back. It bounced. It blew in the wind. It had a life of its own. It had always been this way, and now we were confronted by something completely different.

My sister turned to me and said, in a whisper, "Frankenstein's Mom."

Mom's once lively hair was now held tightly, by glue or something, in a large bundle on the top of her head. There was no way this hair was going to bounce. It was more likely that things would bounce off of it. The wind would have little effect on what appeared to be an immovable mountain of hair, but at least she hadn't changed its color.

Mom smiled at us and asked eagerly, "What do you think?"

I couldn't reply.

My sister said, "Gee, Mom, it's really something,"

but there was a tone in her voice that gave away her true feelings.

Mom said, disappointed, "You don't like it."

My sister, seeing this, said, "No, really, it's nice. It's got great body and, and it's really different."

I nodded in agreement.

Mom said, "Thanks."

Her voice was sad, and we could see that she was hurt. She went into the kitchen and didn't come out.

We thought that perhaps we were just unsophisticated and couldn't appreciate this new style. We were, after all, children. Having seen her reaction to our reaction, we worried about what Dad would think. We hoped that maybe he wouldn't notice. Fat chance.

When Dad got home, we were on pins and needles. We had heard Mom working in the kitchen, but we had been afraid to go in and help her, so we weren't sure how she was. Dad asked us how we were.

My sister looked nervously toward the kitchen and replied, "Fine, just fine."

Dad questioned us with a look, but didn't say

anything. He started for the kitchen.

When he got there, Mom turned and looked at Dad. Dad looked at Mom. No words were spoken. They were both smiling, sort of.

Finally, Dad said, "Honey, your hair."

Mom burst into tears and rushed out of the kitchen. We heard our parents' bedroom door slam.

Dad came out and looked at us.

He sighed deeply, bent down toward us, and said, "Kids, this isn't a real crisis, but it is important. Your Mother is a little sensitive about this. We need to let her know that we love her."

Here he paused and looked down the hallway, thoughtfully. He turned back to us and said, "Even if her hairdo does make her look like Frankenstein's Mom." He stifled a huge laugh in my sister's sweater and then quickly put his finger to his lips and said, "I'll take care of this. It's going to be all right."

Chapter 15

High Stakes

Not many babies feel the urge to gamble; we would rather eat than throw dice. A handful of cards is difficult to manage. We fall asleep in casinos, and the smoke bothers us. And the track is the kind of place where you want to be mobile. It's no fun being dependent on Mom and Dad to run you back and forth from the betting windows.

I didn't know much about gambling that day, in March, when I witnessed a card game between my father and my sister. In the course of that game, I learned many things, some of which have helped me and some things that I would rather forget.

It started out one Saturday afternoon, when my sister asked Mom to play cards with her. Their game was Fish.

Mom was knitting and had come to a particularly crucial point in the sweater she was working on, so she asked my sister to wait a while. From his spot on the couch, my father overheard this request.

He popped up and said, "Little girl, have I ever shown you the card trick for which I am famous?"

My sister looked at Mom, who shrugged.

My sister then said, "Dad, is this like the joke about the insurance salesman?"

My father assured her that this was completely different in that it relied on manual, not verbal and conceptual, prestidigitation. He said he had been shown this trick by none other than Minnesota Fats, during the slightly dissolute youth the two of them had shared in Minneapolis.

My sister, though still skeptical, got the cards and they sat down in the middle of the floor. Dad winked at Mom and made quite a show shuffling the deck. Even I could tell that he had spent some time with them. When he was done, he spread them, with a flourish, on the floor and, by lifting only the last one, flipped the entire deck, turning them, from the single image on the back of each, to face up with their individual markings.

My sister was impressed. She applauded. Mom stomped her feet, and I banged my bottle on the blanket. Dad acknowledged our praise with a smile and a tip of his head. He then had my sister cut the cards seven times. After this, he dealt the cards out into several piles. He kept up a steady patter about playing poker with some guys for big stakes and a lot of other stuff.

The cards were all out, and then he said it was time to show the hands. But first, in his attempt to heighten suspense and to provide enough working knowledge of poker so we could appreciate his trick, he explained a few of the rules and the order of the hands. Royal Flush, Straight Flush, Four of a Kind, Full House, etc.

He turned over the cards of the first imaginary player -- Full House.

"Oooh," he said, "that's going to be hard to beat."

He turned over the second pile of cards -- Full House again. My sister's eyes got bigger. Mom had stopped knitting. Each time he turned the cards over it was a Full House. We couldn't figure it out. There was only his own hand left. He turned it over -- Royal Flush.

It was amazing. We went wild, and Dad modestly pulled the cards together and began shuffling again. He was about to put the deck away and resume his work on the couch, when my sister asked if he would teach her how to play Poker.

He looked at Mom for her okay.

Mom said, "Don't let her fleece you."

Dad laughed, turned to my sister, and said, "Okay kiddo, there are a few things you have to know before we can really play."

He then explained how bets were made, some of the various games of Poker, the art of bluffing, and other fine points. My sister was taking it all in.

Mom continued knitting, and I followed as much of these explanations as I could before I dozed off.

So many details and numerical combinations caused me to glaze over. My sister, however, was completely absorbed and taking notes.

I was startled from my sleep by the sound of coins. As I blinked my way to consciousness, I saw my sister bringing her collection of coins into the room. They were kept in a mayonnaise jar, and the jar was two-thirds full. She set it down on the floor and sat beside it; opposite her was my father. He had taken some change out of his pockets and placed it beside him. He shuffled the cards.

They started out playing Five Card Draw. It was penny ante. My sister picked up her cards and studied them. She looked at my father and examined his face. She bet two. He met the bet. She then said, "Three please." He dealt the cards. He took two. More bets went into the pot. My sister called. Dad placed his cards face up on the floor. He had two pair -- Jacks and Eights. My sister had three Fours. She raked in the pennies.

My father complimented her and congratulated her

on beginner's luck. My sister smiled, but didn't say anything. She shuffled the cards. I looked at her and saw the same look in her eyes that I had seen when she had been talking about the Tooth Fairy. I saw that she found this more interesting and less painful. That was when I began to worry about Dad.

The hands continued, and it seemed like coins were moving back and forth between them without stopping. After half an hour, Dad went to his bedroom for more coins and his wallet. The game went on and on. The sun was beginning to set and although they had been playing for a couple of hours, they showed no signs of stopping. My mother went to the kitchen and brought back sandwiches, carrots, and milk for the players. They barely looked up to thank her.

Mom and I sat to one side and watched. It was as if we were watching strangers. They didn't talk to us, and any kind of light conversation between them had ended long before. Now they made only the mechanical responses required by the game.

My sister held a carrot between her fingers like a

cigar and said, in a voice I couldn't recognize, "I'll see your nickel and raise you twenty cents."

My father didn't look up and shoved two dimes into the pot. To me, the pot looked huge. There must have been over a dollar in it, but neither of them were the least bit uneasy.

If these were poker faces, I didn't want to look at them. They seemed cold, detached, and unforgiving. Mom seemed to feel the same way and suggested that perhaps there had been enough Poker for one day.

My father raised his head and with a distressed look said, shortly, "Just a few more hands."

My sister fiddled with her chips.

The game went on. Mom and I had dinner by ourselves. My sister and father had their sandwiches. It was getting close to bedtime. They had been playing Texas Hold 'Em for the last half hour and, although my father had won a few hands, it was obvious who was winning. There was a pile of loot on my sister's side and almost nothing on my father's. My sister's side even had a few dollar bills.

Dad laughed nervously and seemed desperate. He bet, but his heart wasn't in it.

Mom finally put her foot down and said, "One last hand. It's time for bed."

Dad suggested that my sister fill her jar with coins and then bet what remained on this hand.

My sister said, "Okay, but what are you going to put up?"

Dad looked down at his coins. He had about twenty-three cents. That wasn't going to cut it.

He looked at my sister and said, "I'll put all this in and raise your allowance fifty cents a week."

Mom was shocked, but Dad told her politely to stay out of it.

My sister quickly calculated fifty cents a week for fifty-two weeks and agreed before he could change his mind. Since they were betting everything, they decided that they would cut the cards. The high card would take all.

There was sweat on my father's forehead. My sister looked unconcerned, but I knew her little heart was beating wildly. My father cut first -- Jack of Clubs. He looked up at all of us and smiled for the first time in quite a while. My sister looked at the remaining cards, as if she could see right through them. She then reached down and took half of what was left. She turned it over -- the Queen of Hearts. She let out an unqueenly scream of victory.

My father, who was just beginning to understand the depth of his defeat, went to the kitchen for a cold glass of milk. Mom helped my sister carry her winnings to the room and put us to bed.

Finally, Mom bent over my sister and said wearily, "Your father is a man who knows many things. Today he taught you a lot, some of which is useful, and you proved yourself to be a great student. I just hope he learned his lesson. See you in the morning."

She came over and gave me a weary look, before she kissed me goodnight, and then walked across the room and turned out the light.

Chapter 16

By The Beautiful Sea

Life at our house wasn't all fun and games, sometimes I had to have a bath. Not that I needed one. I was a clean, well-mannered baby. I was fed only a bottle, so there was not much chance of being covered with food. It was too cold to go outside and get dirty, and sitting in a high chair or in a crib you don't work up much of a sweat. Given all that, I just couldn't understand why Mom insisted that I have a bath so often. Of course, I did wear diapers and didn't want a rash, so it was probably a good idea.

It was odd. She didn't have to say a word to me about it. She would be walking toward me, like she had done a million times before, but there would be something in her eye that would tip me off. I knew it was that time. I wasn't sure whether she enjoyed these baths and I hadn't really made up my mind yet, either. There were good things about it, and there were bad.

I want to talk about the bad things first. Mom, in the act of bathing me, had a tendency to revert to the goo, goo, goo talk, and this about drove me crazy. Most of the time, she treated me like a normal member of the family: one who could appreciate jokes, political observations, and direct statements of fact, but it seemed that the combination of my small size and the water set her off. She would be goo, goo, gooing through the whole thing.

Another thing I didn't like about baths was soap. I know this is an essential element and a cleaning substance without peer, but, no matter how careful she was, it seemed to always get into my eyes. And it hurt. A baby's life is a pampered one, and hurt just doesn't figure too much. I cried. I couldn't help it. And then Mom would feel bad and goo, goo, goo even more than she had been.

Baths, although they take place in hot or, at least, warm water, can be quite a cold proposition. No matter how hard you try, there is some part of your body that is not covered by the water. Or has been covered and now isn't. Evaporation takes place, cooling the skin surface. The cool air searches out this recently warm patch of skin and goes to work on it with its icy teeth. I often thought about wearing my clothes when I had a bath, but didn't quite know how to put it to Mom.

Every now and then, while bathing, I would have a fit of modesty. This is not convenient to have when you are being washed by a woman who is six times your size. You are powerless in your tub or bassinet.

Sometimes my sister would walk by and make a joke about my pudgy body. It was embarrassing. What could I do? I was a baby. Babies just are pudgy. We can't work out. We need that flab for something. When these fits hit me, I would sit up suddenly and try to cover myself with my beard. In doing so, I splashed Mom, who would tell me that bathing is hard enough without my squirming and that I should just relax and enjoy it. I tried and, sometimes, it worked.

My astrological sign is Aquarius, the water bearer, and I was determined to bear this water as best I could and even enjoy it, if possible. On the days when everything went right -- no soap in the eyes, the proper temperature, my sister at school -- I sank into the water and, soothed by my mother's meaningless words, drift away.

My eyes closed and, after a few moments, I felt the warmth of the water and begin to hear it gently lap upon the shore. I found that the sand beneath me was better than any blanket. It was heated by a tropical sun that never quit. I could hear the far-off call of the sea birds as they rode the thermals and played tag with the waves and with each other.

On the breeze came a fragrance that was a mixture of pure sea air and the perfume of exotic and colorful orchids, with just a little suntan lotion thrown in. From a grass shack farther up the beach, I could hear the most beautiful and relaxing music. A steel guitar provided a wave of notes on which rode a language that consisted almost entirely of vowels. Wui ooi ooi oo, they sang. Gooey, gooey, gooey, goo. It was that great Hawaiian singer, Baby Pahanui. I stroked my beard in the sunlight and sighed. This was the life.

I thought of my family back home in Minnesota. Dad, at the office, in a business not a bathing suit, making deals right and left. My sister, at school, sitting at a hard desk trying to spell words whose meanings she barely knew. And Mom, slaving away in the kitchen, making a pot roast for her continuously hungry family.

I hoped that someday, when they weren't so busy, they could join me here. Dad could trade coconuts at the market. My sister could learn to Hula and teach French to the natives. And Mom could prepare Ahi and smoothies for dinner. I, of course, would be lying right here on the beach, watching the surf roll in, and humming along to the music. Didn't they say that life was a beach? You just had to find the right one.

I decided that my front side had roasted enough and began to turn over. As I did, I felt, with a shock, the water go up my nose and I spluttered. There is no other word for it. I quickly opened my eyes. Not only was there soap in them, but I also realized that I was still in Minnesota. What a rude awakening.

Mom was laughing and said, "For a guy who doesn't like baths, you were pretty relaxed there."

I smiled at her politely and then tried to close my eyes again, hoping that somehow I could get back to that beach, but it was no good. My eyes stung, my hands were like prunes, and I was cold. The tropics were a long ways away from this icebox.

Mom said, "Wait a minute," and turned to get my favorite towel.

It was large and a beautiful blue, like the ocean. She picked me up out of the water and laid me on the towel. It was warm, right out of the dryer. She folded me in it and held me close. I sighed and closed my eyes. I could almost hear the music.

Chapter 17

Dad Meets Mom

One afternoon we were all lying around the living room. All of us, except Mom. She was somewhere else. Out with The Girls or at the store. My sister, who I knew had been waiting for just the right moment, asked Dad how he had met Mom. Dad was surprised.

He blushed and said, "Oh, you know, we met, fell in love, and got married."

My sister said, "I know that, but how, where, when?"

Dad realized there was no way out of this and understood that he would never be able to return to his research on the couch, until he told her. He leaned back, looked at us, a receptive audience, and said, "Okay, here's the story."

"When I was a young man going to college back east, times were tough. The depression was on, and money was scarce. I studied business and was determined that when I got out of school, I would know how to make a living so that I could buy you two lots of presents. I was a serious young man and always had a job while I went to school. In the summers, I was a lifeguard at the beach.

"The beach was the big hangout, and all the kids were there each day. From my perch, in the chair, I could see thousands of young people up and down the beach. They were getting tan, playing, running, swimming, and talking. There were groups of guys talking about their cars and money and what they were going to do next week. There were also groups of girls who talked about whatever girls talked about - their mothers, fashion, sewing. Who knows? At night there were parties on the beach, but after a full day of lifeguarding, I was too tired for that. I always went back to my room, studied, and went to bed early.

"My job, as lifeguard, was to pay attention to what

was happening out in the water, not on the beach. Most days, the most exciting thing that happened was that someone got sunburned and that was fine with me. I'd watch the people swimming and I'd watch the waves roll in and I kept a lookout for sharks. That's right. Sharks. No one had actually seen one at this beach in eight years, but the possibility kept me on my toes.

"Every now and then, someone would swim too far out from shore and I would race out there and help them in. Or, someone's dog was a better swimmer than they were, but had a weak sense of direction, and I'd go out and get them, too. Once in a while, something serious happened, a near drowning, and my fellow lifeguards and I would do everything we could to save someone. In the three years I worked there, no one died. Thank God. But we did have some close calls.

"One day, I was scanning the water and noticed someone out there, much farther than they should have been. This swimmer was way past the markers.

I got up on my chair and attempted to wave him in. Of course, he didn't see me. He didn't look like he was in trouble, so I decided I would keep my eye on him until he came in and then I would go down and let him have it. This kind of thing was dangerous and really made me angry.

"As I watched this guy, I thought I saw something moving even farther out than he was. Maybe it was just a wave, but it made me nervous. All of a sudden, my stomach turned over as I realized that it might be a shark. I used my binoculars and saw, to my horror, that this was much worse than any shark. This object moving toward the swimmer so quickly was a deadly, giant squid.

"I jumped from my chair, strapped my knife to my leg, and plunged into the water. I tore out away from the safety of shore. The water was freezing. I passed the markers in mere seconds and headed for the thrashing water ahead of me.

"When I got there, I found that the Squid had one long, creepy, tentacle wrapped around the body of the swimmer and held him, for a moment, high above the water. I was shocked to see that it wasn't a man, it was your mother. She wasn't your mother then. At that point, I had never even met her.

"The Squid saw me with its huge, bulging eyes. I shouted at it to let her go and pulled my knife and placed it between my teeth. I swam toward it. The Squid tossed your mother to one side and turned to face me. In the seconds before it attacked, I had the consoling thought that, at least, she was safe. Then there was no time for thinking. A slimy tentacle wrapped itself around my middle and pulled me to the oozing body of the Squid. If he could have, he would have thrown his head back and laughed. He was sure he had me in his power.

"I could hear your mother's screams, and I thought, whatever I do, I have to save her from this monster. I took my knife from my teeth and shouted to her to swim to shore. I barely got that out, before I was pulled, suddenly, beneath the water. Luckily, my arms were still free, and I began to attack the Squid with my knife. It was like going after a Grizzly with a toothpick, but it was all I had.

"I knew that if I could strike a sensitive place, the Squid might be stunned enough to release me. I stabbed repeatedly, but nothing happened. The noise was incredible. The water thrashed about me, and my heart pounded desperately. My breath was almost gone, but worry would do me no good. I could only keep hitting the Squid and hope that I would get lucky. Time slowed, and our struggle seemed to go on forever. Things started to look pretty bleak. My strength began to desert me.

"Suddenly I was being lifted from the water. I looked down and saw the black cavern of the Squid's giant jaws waiting for me. I knew I had only one chance, and I threw my knife with every ounce of strength that remained. It went straight into the cold, cruel eye of the beast and there was a terrible sound -- part thunder and part cry of agony.

"The next thing I knew, I was flying through the air and hit the water on my back with a force that knocked the wind out of me. A wave of panic shot through me, and then everything went black. Seconds later, I regained consciousness and realized that your mother was with me and that she was holding my head above water. Our battle was over. We were both safe. As we looked out to sea, we saw the mass that had been the Squid sink slowly into the icy depths. Your mother and I then helped each other back to shore and, as they say, the rest is history."

My sister and I, as you can imagine, were on the edge of our seats and breathless after this story. It was so amazing.

After a few moments my sister managed to say, "But Mom told us a story about how you met that was completely different."

My father simply looked at her and said, "Well, you know how it is, women are such romantics."

Chapter 18

Watch The Birdie

Mom had decided that we should be in pictures. Not the movies, although that's where my sister wanted to be and where I thought we belonged, but Mom meant that she wanted to have portraits made of us. A record, she said, of what we looked like right now. Right now, early Friday morning, Dad was in his boxers searching for his brown pants, and my sister's eyes didn't quite seem to match. I felt pretty peppy, but I couldn't vouch for my appearance. Mom, of course, looked wonderful.

Dad said, "Sure, maybe later," and my sister nodded vaguely.

Mom said she wanted us to go to the studio to get our photographs taken. Formal portraits, she said, and we had an appointment for 10:00 tomorrow.

Dad thought of an important project on the couch that he had scheduled at that time, but said, "That will be great, dear."

My sister, on general principles, groaned.

I was excited. This meant getting out of the house, and that meant adventure. I also liked the idea of having my picture taken. It was a kind of confirmation of my standing, well, let's say my position, in the family. It would be a moment frozen in time and, not just any moment, but that particular moment, and everything I had been and everything I was and maybe everything I would become would be fixed in that picture and revealed to me and to the world. It would be a document, a discovery, a statement of personality. I took a breath. I had to calm down. I was getting a little too excited.

Dad and my sister went off to their world, and Mom and I stayed behind and cleaned up the kitchen. Actually, Mom cleaned, I watched. All morning I thought about our appointment the next day, and

I practiced poses the entire afternoon, trying different ones out and wondering which might be the best.
Mom was looking at me kind of funny as I did this.
I suppose it looked to her like I had indigestion, but
when I stuck my hand between the buttons on my
chest, in imitation of a military leader my sister idol-
ized, she understood.

She smiled at me and said, "That's the spirit, big guy."

The next morning, Mom needed to use all her skills
to get us ready. She laid out all of my father's clothes
so that he would be on time. She then began the
production that was my sister. They brushed, they
combed, they tied, they buttoned, and, finally, she was
done. Even I thought she looked great -- no ugly
barrettes, no ugly socks. Mom put me in my best
outfit and brushed my beard until it had the shape of
a lion's mane. It shone in the sunlight.

She made us line up in the kitchen and took a good
look at us. Now that the preparation was over and
we were really going, my sister and my father began
to smile a bit. Mom put on her coat, bundled me up,

and conducted us all to the car. Mom drove. No one said a word. Her driving was an adventure in itself, but that's another story. All I can say now is that we made it to the studio.

The studio was a small place run by a short man with a Scandinavian accent. There was an entrance with a desk and a woman who answered the phone. We were ushered past her into the back. The back had a split personality. One end of the room was all business -- concrete, ladders, lights, cameras, and equipment. The other end was soft chairs, curtains, and pillows. We got the good end.

The photographer went for my mother first. The rest of us were recovering from the drive. She smiled confidently, as he snapped away. Every now and then, he adjusted the lights and he smiled at my mother, as he did so. Next, he posed my father. Seated at a desk, my father looked off into the distance, while in his hand he held, no doubt, some important contract.

Dad, despite his earlier reluctance, was warming to this occasion and suggested a standing pose. This was soon accomplished. The photographer was ready for my sister, but my father thought that, just to cover all bases, there should be one of him relaxing in a chair. He also thought that the light wasn't hitting his face quite right and said so. The photographer adjusted the lights noisily and snapped three pictures right in a row, hardly giving Dad a chance to perfect his pose.

He then, immediately, said, "And now for Mademoiselle."

My sister, of course, thrilled to these words, and somewhat dramatically took her place beneath the lights. He kept telling her to relax, but she had her own ideas of how things should be. On her face was an expression I had never seen before. It seemed that the photographer had never seen one like it, either. He began muttering to himself behind the camera.

Finally, it was my turn. Mom placed me in a chair that was just my size. Evidently, the photographer had forgotten that I had a beard, because when he came toward me to adjust the pose, he stopped suddenly and put his hand to his forehead. He shook his head, as if to clear it, and asked me to hold still. I wanted to show him some of the poses I had worked on, but he wasn't interested.

He said in a strained tone, "Just hold still."

I thought he probably hadn't had a good night's sleep and I tried my best to cooperate. He went back to the camera and, in baby talk, said, "Watch the birdie." This baby talk stuff was beginning to get on my nerves and, despite my intentions, I wasn't smiling. Mom whispered something to him. He looked at her, shrugged, and said, in a completely different voice, "Young man, smile please." That was better. A couple more like that and he was done with me.

The time had come for our picture, as a family, to be taken. The photographer relaxed a little, knowing that the session was almost over. We were posed on a couch with my sister sitting next to my father and me resting in Mom's lap. We adjusted our positions on the couch. We smoothed our clothes and our hair. We cleared our throats and put forth our best smiles. Just as the shutter clicked, my father reached toward his head to check on his hair.

Behind the camera, the photographer straightened himself quickly, looked at us, and said quietly, "Once more, please, and, this time, no moving."

We were silent and ready. He said, "One, two, three." On three, two things happened. He snapped the picture, and my sister sneezed like I had never heard her before. He let out a small noise, came out toward this family scene, and blinked rapidly at us, unbelieving. We prepared ourselves again. This time, much to my shame, I have to admit that I burped violently, at the worst possible moment. The photographer was beside himself.

He said, "Really!" as if he really meant it and tried to stare us into submission.

Mom called a family huddle and we determined that this would be the one. We had barely returned to our positions, let alone actually posed, when we heard the shutter click.

The photographer was smiling now and as he

hurried toward us, with our coats, he said, "That was perfect. What a handsome family."

Chapter 19

TV or Not TV

We considered ourselves a
modern family. We had electricity, running water, and
those kinds of things. We had an automobile. Dad
read in *Popular Mechanics* about the homes of the
future and about inventions that would allow everyone
to sleep until eleven o'clock. Mom had her hair done
by professionals, my sister went to a modern school,
and I drank my modern formula, daily.

Things, in general, were good in this modern world,
but our family was deficient in one area -- we didn't
have a television. It was a fairly new development,
and we had never had one. Everyone was talking about it and about the people they saw on it. It
seemed many important things were happening in this

television world -- Cowboys were fighting Indians, refrigerators were being given away, queens were being crowned daily, jokes were being told, news was being reported. In fact, just about everything was happening there. Our family knew nothing about it.

Dad brought the television home with him one evening. He said they were giving them away. Mom said she doubted this, and Dad admitted that he had it on a three-day trial. He called it a TV. He placed the TV in the living room, and we all stared at it. This turned out to be all we would ever do, but we didn't know that then. It didn't look like much. The wood cabinet was nice and so were the knobs, but the glass picture screen was a dull green and made the whole thing seem cold. But then, we turned it on.

It was like magic. Our mouths hung open. My sister squealed. Mom was fascinated. Dad was turning the volume up and down and I wondered who the guy on the screen was. Dad flicked through the channels. There were four of them. This meant endless variety.

We sat right down and went to work, so to speak.

We watched a show where people were singing. The men looked fashionable with their tight little jackets and their shiny hair. The women all had very black lips. From lots of lipstick, Mom said. Their dresses were huge and stuck almost straight out. The people on TV danced together as they sang and as they did, Mom and Dad got up and joined them.

My sister and I were amazed. We had no idea our parents were so talented and so graceful. They twirled and glided through each number. They were laughing and whispering to one another. It seemed they had forgotten all about us and all about the TV.

My sister came over and picked me up. She danced me around the room murmuring phrases in French. That was how we spent our first evening with television -- dancing through commercials for soap and through whatever else appeared.

The next day, my sister and I, upon waking, went directly to the set. She turned it on and the program she settled on was called, All-Star Wrestling. Guys in swimming suits were in a ring throwing each other around. The crowd around the ring looked small, and the place was dark. There was a lot of noise, but neither of us said much. We watched, as if hypnotized. I'm not sure how long we sat there, but we saw a succession of matches. One even had women fighting, and another had midgets. We had never seen midgets before. Mom and Dad came in and watched with us.

In the beginning, it was kind of exciting. It was new. It was funny. My sister suggested that Mom join the show as a wrestler, and Mom flexed her muscles. As time went on, the shows changed. Between shows we waved to each other, as if we hadn't seen one another in a long time or as if we were passing on the street. It was odd, because we didn't talk. We checked to make sure we were all there, and then we turned back to the TV and were immediately caught up in the next program.

All of a sudden, Mom stood up and said, "Look at the time. We forgot dinner."

Forgot dinner?! That was impossible. We ate like an army. Our appetites were always restless. We would no more forget about eating than we would forget about breathing. And yet, Mom was right. We were all shocked by this. My sister and I were also shocked by how late it was. Wasn't it just afternoon? What had happened to us? Mom brought us out slices of cold meatloaf and Velveeta and glasses of milk and we ate, as the shows rolled on.

There were people riding on bicycles in circles on a stage and jumping on and off. During this, my sister looked over at me as if to say, "Our next mission." Then, an old woman was talking to a dog and it looked like the dog was talking back.

Later, a movie came on. It was a prison movie, and all the prisoners were women. Mom changed the channel to another movie. This one had cars chasing each other at night. Everything was dark in this movie, and it was hard to tell what was really going on, even when the people in it talked. They all had names like Lefty or Louie or Susan.

It was fascinating to me, and I took it all in, but, as the night went on, I saw my entire family fall asleep. Right there in the living room. Dad was the first to go. Lefty was talking to Louie, and his face was about an inch from Louie's rather big nose, when I heard a snort. At first, I thought it was Louie, but then I realized that it was Dad, on the couch. His arm was covering his eyes and I knew that was it for him. Mom was next. She had been sitting in a big chair knitting while she watched. I looked over during one of the commercials and saw that she had pulled the yarn about her like a blanket and her head was on her chest. Her breathing was deep and regular.

My sister was on the floor and, when I looked at her, it was obvious that she had been out for a while. She was lying on her stomach, next to her dinner plate, and some of her hair had fallen into the ketchup. I turned my attention to the screen. Lefty was pounding Louie in the face with his fists. After he finished this, there was a shot of Susan bending over Louie. She looked up and said, "You're a brute, Lefty. An animal." That's all I remember.

I was startled awake by a shriek. It didn't come from the TV. It came from my mother. I looked at her, and she was shaking Dad on the couch. It appeared the sun had just come up. I looked at the screen and saw that it showed only a test pattern. Mom had calmed down by now and made sure that we were all awake. She turned off the TV and stood before it. She had our attention.

She said, "Well, we've had our TV trial. And it seems to have been a success. No one got any exercise, we didn't talk to one another, we forgot dinner, and we even forgot to go to bed. We saw women in prison, midget wrestlers, a woman talking to a dog, and someone who won a Hoover. Life is short. Is this how we want to spend our time?"

Dad took the TV back that day, and no one ever mentioned it again. We went back to the things we had done before and found that they were more exciting than guys on bikes or cars chasing each other. It wasn't that we were old-fashioned; we just didn't want to be that modern.

Chapter 20

If 6 Were 9

My sister wasn't getting any younger. In fact, each day, each month, each year, she was getting older. From her perspective, this was a good thing. She didn't really believe that you started to live until you were at least nineteen and able to go to Paris and fall in love. Falling in love simply wasn't possible in Minnesota, especially if you were a little kid.

When one was nineteen and in love and in Paris, one sat at cafes all day and then drank champagne and danced until dawn. One rode around with tall, dark strangers whose accents were perfect and whose fingernails were always clean. One walked barefoot, with these strangers in evening clothes, through the park in the hour before dawn and, while everyone else slept, the hem of one's dress became soaked with dew. When in Paris, you never slept.

Eating in Paris was something that consisted entirely of plates of croissants and mugs of strong coffee laced with absinthe. What free hours one had were spent writing billet doux and planning revolutions. Every now and then, one would pose for a famous painter who was trying to capture the immediacy of youth and who would record your beauty and spirit for all of time.

The conversation in Paris was brilliant, and no one ever said anything as boring as, "Hey, how about this weather?" and if, by chance, they did, they at least said it in French, which made it sound romantic and exciting. The French weren't concerned about the state of their lawns or about going to school. They were concerned with the romantic possibilities of the moment. Their joie de vivre made it impossible to do the laundry or wash the dishes. Glasses were always dashed into the fireplace after passionate pledges concerning devotion and honor. And plates and silverware too, after dinners too elaborate and too subtle to describe, which only a French chef could create.

Duels to the death were common and were fought, at the drop of a hat, to defend one's personal honor or that of a lady. And young women were weeping, as a result, all the time, but it was said that they were soon comforted. Time beat to a different rhythm in Paris -- one lived, one loved, one died. It was so tragic and, yet, so beautiful.

These were the kinds of things my sister told me, in the dark, as we waited for sleep. These were her dreams. This was what she lived for. How she found out about all this was a mystery to me. Neither Mom nor Dad had ever been to France. The only French my father knew was, "C'est moi," which he said rather too often and to which my mother would always respond, "Mais oui." This was not a lot to go on, but somehow my sister kept these dreams alive and waited for the day when she would be old enough to make them real.

I worried a little about her, but it did seem wonderful and romantic, and I never heard of anyone's sister dying in a duel. Maybe it was the prospect of dueling or maybe the clean fingernails that kept me from sharing these dreams, but I knew that this kind of life was not for me. My future lay elsewhere. Maybe right here in Minnesota. It seemed to me that there was plenty of time, but not for my sister. She wanted it now. She wanted to hurry time to accommodate her wishes.

This was why my sister tried to convince our parents to let her have a birthday every three months. Even three months was a long time to her, but she was determined to prove that she was more mature and more patient than they thought. She reasoned that with a birthday every three months, she would be ready to go to Paris in about three years. That would give her enough time to save her money and perfect her French. She was a practical girl and didn't want to arrive at the adventure of a lifetime unprepared.

This proposed change in birthdays was something

that caught Mom and Dad by surprise, and they nodded thoughtfully as they listened to her argument.

Dad said, "What an interesting idea."

Mom said, "Mais oui," which made my sister smile. Mom went on to say, "May we take a couple of days and think it over?"

My sister said sure, there was plenty of time. But she didn't really mean it because, to her, each minute of indecision was a minute stolen from her future. A future of romance and adventure, which had nothing to do with something so tiresome as deliberating over whether birthdays happened every three or every twelve months. In her future, decisions were to be made immediately, not to say impulsively.

My sister suffered this period of waiting with the forbearance of Joan of Arc, which meant she alternated between storming around the room and quiet moments of prayer. She tried to make up for any previous bad behavior by helping Mom in the kitchen and by discussing the stock market with Dad. She was polite at the table and didn't spill anything.

While, most of the time, she would parade her good behavior and good judgement before Mom and Dad, every now and then she would come over to where I was and wink and hold up her hands, which had all of their fingers crossed. She would shake them excitedly, for emphasis, and then calmly smooth her hair and gracefully glide back to help Mom clear the table or to discuss price-earnings ratios with Dad.

Finally, a family meeting was called. It was thought best that I be present because birthdays were a big deal in our house and affected everyone. They also thought that, young as I was, I might have ideas of my own concerning getting older. It had been decided that Dad would speak.

This is what he said: "Children, for many years, your mother and I have felt that birthdays were entirely too arbitrary. I mean, consider that, just for example of course, one could one day be a somewhat contented thirty-nine years old and the next be a declining forty. It just doesn't seem fair."

He paused.

He looked at my sister and said, "In your case, time stretches out in front of you in a slow-as-molasses accumulation, which keeps you from realizing your dreams. That doesn't seem fair either. We've thought about it a lot these last two days, and I can assure you that I have personally agonized about the whole issue quite recently. And so, with your assistance and agreement, we propose that, for the practical purpose of maintaining the peace of mind of all family members, we will celebrate your birthday every three months and we will celebrate ours every three years."

My sister was overjoyed. This changed everything. Her brain began, at once, to calculate the future. Mom was smiling, and Dad looked as if years had been lifted from his shoulders.

My sister's expression changed and she said, "That means that, at some point, we will all meet at the same age."

That seemed like a great idea to me.

She went on in a somewhat different voice, "But then, I will get even older than you guys are and I will be aging faster."

She sighed and stood up. It was clear she was beginning to have second thoughts.

Chapter 21

On The Road

Behind the wheel, Mom was like a different person. It was as if all of her maternal characteristics fled in fear when she was driving. If she could have changed her shape to match her behavior, she would have shrunk down, filled out, had a cap pulled down over bushy eyebrows, smoked a cigar, and would have slouched severely.

The closest Mom ever got to swearing, with the exception of an occasional 'Hell's bells', was when she was driving. There, she refrained for our sake, but she did put forth a constant stream of commentary about everything -- animate and inanimate. If a traffic light turned red at an inopportune moment, she had some words for it and for the people who manufactured it and for the poor guys who installed it.

If the person driving the car in front of her was going too slow for her liking, she told him so and went on to question the value of his existence and his place of origin. If a pedestrian made any move toward the lane she was driving in, she laid on the horn and made signals with her hands, which were meant to put him back in his place.

When Mom drove, she slapped the dashboard. She hit the side of the car. She muttered, she criticized, she yelled. Her face would change colors with the lights. She was never at peace, but she enjoyed every minute of it.

Her own driving, surprisingly, was very good. She wasn't reckless, although she wasn't slow. She always let other cars into her lane, if they had signaled properly and waved politely. She stopped at the lights, which was more than some people did. She was a defensive driver. Her reactions were quick and, when called upon, her head proved cool in emergencies. She had never had an accident.

If she hadn't been a Mom, I think she might have become a truck driver. I can see her now, sitting high above the highway in a big eighteen-wheeler. Her T-shirt is rolled up over her bulging biceps and on the door, in flashy letters, it reads "Ma -- Minneapolis, Minnesota." She's on the CB comparing notes with her fellow truckers, making jokes about the hats that those State Patrol boys wear and how they probably couldn't shift out of automatic, if their lives depended on it. I hate to say it, but, at this point, Mom spits out the window for emphasis.

She's humming "Six Days on the Road" and eating up the miles between Minneapolis and Great Falls. She pulls into a truck stop, every five hours or so, and has a half gallon of coffee and some doughnuts and then helps the waitress clear the counter and the booths over by the window.

Yes, it's an independent life and, except for the tourists in their overloaded Fords and Chevys, the road belongs to her and to the other professionals, who follow their own code and drive off into the sunset, whenever they feel like it.

But as much as Mom liked to drive, she didn't get much opportunity to do so. For one thing, Dad wouldn't let her. He said things about his being old enough already and how he thought she was doing too much all the time and how he would like to do something for her. He'd just go out and warm up the car. He also said things like, 'what about the children?' Plus, he made sure he always had the keys. Even though Mom was safety itself, his nerves and ours just couldn't take it.

As a passenger, Mom was her same old self, which meant polite, cheerful, kind, attractive, and motherly. You might think she would try to tell my father or, at least, the other drivers on the road how to do things, but she never did. Dad and she had worked this out long before I came along. Although she didn't say so, it made her sad that she didn't drive very much. She missed the independence of it and the friendly inter-action with the other drivers.

One night, at dinner, she brought up the subject.

It was mostly directed at Dad, but she told all of us that she had changed. She no longer had to or would drive the way she had in the past. She had turned over a new leaf. She really had, and there was nothing more to worry about. Her actions on the road would be above reproach and beyond censure. She said she knew there was no reason to get upset behind the wheel and that those days were gone forever. From now on, while driving, she would be the soul of kindness and the image of sweetness.

Dad listened to this in silence. He looked to us for assistance. He looked back at Mom. She was quiet now and smiling, waiting.

My sister said, "Dad, give her a chance. You know she's a good driver."

Dad seemed doubtful. I nodded my support.

He thought for a moment, turned to Mom and said, "Okay, Honey."

The next day, we all drove to the store together. Mom was at the wheel. My sister was in the back, and I was on Dad's lap in front. The three of us were holding our breath, and we looked back and forth from the road to Mom to see how things were. Mom seemed fine, and everything was okay. We stopped at the lights, we changed lanes, we parked at the store.

On our way home, Dad was smiling. He really didn't enjoy driving the way Mom did and was pleased to be back in the role of passenger. He was glad that he had given her a chance and that things had worked out so well. Just then, when everything seemed different, a car cut in front of us and made a quick turn into a driveway. Mom was forced to slam on the brakes to avoid hitting it. She immediately pulled over to the side of the road and turned off the car. She looked at us, smiled, and said quietly, "Excuse me." She then got out of the car.

Our eyes followed her, and as she passed in front of the car, she seemed to become shorter, fatter. There was a cap on her head and a cigar in her left hand. She slouched up to the car that had cut in front of us. Its driver was just getting out. We heard a voice that couldn't have been Mom's, but we saw that the other guy was listening. The voice went on and on.

Dad covered his face with his hands and sighed. My sister and I looked out the rear window and tried to think of something else. Finally, the door opened, and Mom climbed in and started the engine. We stared at her. She arranged her dress, smiled sweetly at us, and pulled smoothly into traffic. The blinker of our Ford and the beating of our hearts were the only sounds we heard.

Chapter 22

Mr. Fixit

My father didn't have a mechanical bone in his body. He was not good with tools. In fact, with tools he became dangerous. Anything more complex than a pencil and Dad became a menace to whatever he was working on and to all of those around him. When something broke at our house, it stayed that way. Despite evidence to the contrary, Dad insisted he would get around to it sometime.

He was not the kind of father who had a workshop with all the tools neatly placed within their outline on the wall. He was not building bookshelves, in the basement, in his spare time. He certainly had no plans for adding on a garage or for building a porch on the west side of the house. If he did, we would all have to leave home.

Once, Dad attempted to change a washer on the sink in the bathroom. He had assured my mother that this was a simple operation, involving no power tools and requiring very limited technical knowledge -- the perfect job for him. By the end of the day, my father had still not changed the washer, but he had received a lesson in humility and six stitches in his finger when the screwdriver had slipped. Not only that, but the bathroom had flooded when he removed the cold water knob and it spilled out and soaked the carpet in the hall. The faucet still drips.

Dad had many other talents that made up for this lack of manual dexterity and common mechanical sense. For instance, he was a whiz at business. Give that guy an adding machine and a phone and there was no stopping him. He also appreciated music, drama of all sorts, and good and bad literature. He was wise and fair in the dispensation of justice in domestic matters. He knew two jokes. He was well versed in the history of baseball. He loved animals, and he loved us. With all that, we didn't care that he could barely change a light bulb or that he used a hammer to fix whatever was not functioning properly.

However, he wasn't completely at a loss. He knew how to work the toaster and the few household appliances we had, except for the vacuum cleaner. He could operate the lawn mower without cutting off his foot, although I don't think he ever changed the oil. He drove the car without incident and could mix drinks in the blender. He wasn't a renaissance man, but that didn't make him a bad one.

When something didn't work properly or had broken down, he always made a sincere effort to discover the problem and fix it. He would lie down in front of whatever was not working and study it. Sometimes for hours.

It would seem that he had fallen asleep, but then, just when Mom was about to place a blanket on him, he would jump up and say, "I think I've got it."

Mom would say, "I think he's got it."

My sister would join in, "By George, he's got it."

They'd dance around for a while and, then, Dad would tinker. He would, finally, flick the switch, or whatever, but, sad to say, nothing he fixed ever worked. Because of this, we kept the number of things we had in the house with moving parts to a bare minimum. We tried to enjoy a simple life.

To his credit, he was methodical. On good days, he studied instruction manuals or the How-To Home Repair books that he kept down in his den, but not try to actually do anything. On bad days, he took the problem object apart and its pieces would be neatly arranged on the floor for days. Then Mom would have to put it back together, while he was at work. She could usually fix most things, but didn't, out of consideration for my father's self-respect.

He felt, as head of the household, as a father, and, as a man, that it was his duty to fix these things himself. He felt that he should intuitively know how every-thing worked. He was reluctant to consider calling in a plumber or an electrician or even an odd-jobs kind of guy. Mom tried to humor him, but worried terribly when something involving electricity, fire, or water went on the blink. And yet, he always bravely went ahead and made the effort.

This winter, our hot water heater had been making disturbing noises. Gurgling, moaning, exploding -- it seemed it had acute indigestion. After our initial reactions to this, we ignored the noises and acted as if they were part of its normal operation. That was fine until the morning that my sister started screaming in the bathroom. Mom and Dad rushed to the door expecting something horrible. It turned out that there was no hot water, but that was horrible enough.

My father tested the water himself and agreed with my sister's assessment. Mom suggested we call the plumber, immediately. My father told us all to remain calm; he would handle it. Mom didn't say anything, but it was obvious she thought that hot water, in our house, might permanently become a thing of the past. She went to the kitchen for coffee.

Dad went to his den and consulted his books. They mentioned noises just like the ones we had heard and recommended draining the tank. Draining the tank, in winter in Minnesota, involved finding a hose that wasn't frozen and attaching it to the heater and running it out the door into the freezing cold to drain. My father followed the directions, but somehow nothing came out. He consulted some more. He fiddled, he jiggled, he got out his hammer.

He decided against the hammer and decided to check the pilot light. Sure enough, it was out. Dad consulted his books again. He lay down in front of the water heater and studied it. My sister mentioned that she was freezing. Dad told her that this was Minnesota and one must wear clothes. He studied some more. He was bringing all his powers of concentration and all his hours of study for just such an emergency, to bear on the problem at hand.

Mom brought me from the kitchen, and my sister emerged fully dressed from the bedroom. We gathered around my father and watched as he delicately removed the panel at the base of the heater. The silence was complete with the exception of our tense breathing. Dad looked up and smiled. He had an expression of confidence on his face that informed the one word he spoke, "Matches."

My mother handed them to him without comment. Her hand shook, as she reflected that this operation involved two of the three dreaded elements -- fire and water. As my father took the matches, my sister blurted out, "By George, he's got it," but Mom shushed her. Dad lit the match, turned the knobs at the base of the heater, and plunged his hand into the darkness.

Nothing happened. Dad lit another match and this time there was a whoosh and Dad quickly drew his hand back. The hair on his knuckles was gone, but we knew from the look on his face that we were back in business.

Mom congratulated my father on his success, and my sister said, "You're the greatest," and began peeling off her clothes. Dad smiled modestly and walked toward the kitchen looking somehow taller. A confidence showed in his walk that hadn't been there before.

He said, to no one in particular, "Maybe we should get a dishwasher."

Chapter 23

My Oration

I was a baby of few words. It wasn't that there was nothing to say, there was plenty. It's just that it took me a while to coordinate everything. My mouth was too small. My tongue was too large. I drooled all the time, and my cheeks were so fat that I could barely move them.

Another reason was that I was a thoughtful baby. Having a beard at birth gave me a lot to think about. What did it mean? Why me? It seemed like more than just an accident of birth. More than some caprice of the gods. More than just a lot of hair. It was significant and yet, I felt like a normal baby with normal thoughts, needs, and desires. The more I thought about it, the less I knew, so I decided to let it go.

Someday, perhaps, it would become clear to me.

As a baby, you can't simply start blabbing away. You have to get used to the language and get a feel for meaning, inflection, sentence structure, and the like. You need to assemble a vocabulary that can serve your thoughts. Maybe, if I had been a French baby, it would have been easier, but English was my language, and I was glad of it. Everyone around me spoke it, and it seemed to have endless possibilities. I was a quick learner. This was fine with me, because I felt that if I could speak and communicate, my world would expand, and I might be able to get something to eat besides that formula.

But I wanted to be able to really express myself clearly, before I started talking. I guess that was an extreme position to take, but I didn't want to start out with something as boring as Da Da or ball or horsie. That was too much like Mom's goo, goo, goo. I was proud, and I wanted my family to be proud of me. I was afraid that if I just imitated animal noises or something, they would think that not only did they have a baby with a beard, but that maybe they had one who was dumb, too.

My parents spoke beautifully, and my mother could even sing, which seemed like a language in itself. I often wondered what my voice would sound like and, as the weeks went on, I began to make noises. I experimented with the vowels. When no one was looking and, more importantly, when no one was listening, I would attempt an "AAAA..." I'd draw it out. I'd try it in short, sharp bursts, "A. A. A. A." I'd try it soft and I'd try it loud, but not loud enough to attract attention or to bring Mom to investigate.

I went on to the other vowel sounds - e, i, o, u, and sometimes y. My y sounded more like "Waaa," but I kept practicing. U was my favorite, although I have to admit that, when I first started, it was more "oooo" than the proper "you." I could spend the whole afternoon, in perfect contentment, going "ooo" in continually changing volume, duration, and inflection.

Alone in my crib, I practiced whenever I had a spare moment. I hummed the tunes that I had heard from the record player and the radio and try to sing along. My favorite was "Chattanooga Choo Choo" and, when I got to the end, I would imitate the train's whistle. I tried out other songs and bits of conversation that I had heard.

After the months of listening to everyone, I felt I had a fair grasp of things. I held imaginary conversations in my head, and they seemed to make sense. I narrated events, just to keep in practice: "Mom is on her way to the refrigerator. She is opening the door. She is removing the milk." That sort of thing.

I wanted my first actual words to my family to be something special. I wanted to say something that might be profound, without seeming pretentious. I wanted it to be a true expression of my feelings about them and about my position and role among them.

I began to make up a speech in my head. I would address them in a strong, but not booming, voice and say, "Ladies and Gentleman, in my short time among you..." and so forth. I tried to outline my thoughts. It would have been easier if I could have written it down, but that was asking a little too much.

I also began to consider what might be the perfect time and place for my speech. I settled on a mealtime because I was sure that we would all be together then. Lunch didn't seem to have quite the impact of breakfast or dinner. An after-dinner speech appealed to me, but they might be tired at the end of the day and after a big meal, and I wanted them to hear every word. On the other hand, they weren't always awake at breakfast. It was a dilemma.

One night before bed, we were in the living room. Dad was reading the paper and Mom was knitting. My sister was sprawled on the carpet with a drawing pad and her crayons in front of her. I was in my crib, practicing. I was mumbling the first part of what I had titled, "My Oration."

My sister had finished her picture and took it to Dad for his opinion.

He was in the middle of an article but looked at the picture and said, "Very nice. What is it?"

My sister said, "Oh, Dad," and brought the picture

to my mother, who studied it for a long time.

Mom said, a little uncertainly, "I love the colors," but that was all.

My sister was frustrated and, all of a sudden, the picture was thrust before my face.

"And you, wise guy, what about you?" she said.

Surprised by her question and having my mind on my speech, I looked at it quickly and said, "It's beautiful. Especially the rainbow."

My sister gasped and yelled, "Mom," but both Mom and Dad had heard and were on their way toward me. As soon as the words left my mouth, I knew that that was the end of my oration. My plans were in shambles.

The three of them looked down on me from their grown-up height with amazement, and I smiled, sheepishly, up at them. Maybe it was just as well. I might have flubbed the speech. I took a deep breath and, before I said anything else, I had a feeling that as great as everything had been, it was going to be even greater from now on.

Wonderful World Publishing

www.wonderfulworldpublishing.com